Praise for *You*

'...*You* deserves to find a place in our pantheon of much-admired, beautifully crafted variations on a theme.' Arminta Wallace, *The Irish Times*

'...timeless, placeless and universal... a must read.' Yvonne Hogan, *The Irish Independent*

'...a vivid and immediate sensory experience,...Ní Chonchúir's ear – as you might expect of a poet – is alive to the language of her characters... it is about the ordinary, and the secret life that runs beneath it.' Kevin Power, *The Sunday Business Post*

'The novel flows beautifully and is understated in tone...This gem is sure to win her further acclaim. Nuala Ní Chonchúir is a writer to watch.' Sue Leonard, *The Irish Examiner*

'*You* supplies a pitch-perfect voice to the estranged youngster within each of us, the result being a quietly disarming experience for the reader...It is another success from a writer who seems composed of something that literary awards like to be around... It's all done organically, the hand of the author combining with the reader's own sense of childhood nostalgia to create literary alchemy.' Hilary A. White, *Sunday Independent*

'Ní Chonchúir is excellent on the shifting allegiances between children...this would not have been taken for a début.' Tom Widger, *Sunday Tribune*

'...this novel uses plain prose, vivid detail, fresh images, and the delightful Dublin vernacular. *You* is a compelling story that brings to life complex characters and delivers hard-hitting truths.' Ethel Rohan, *Pank*

'Her prose is both dignifying and empowering to her subjects, and it is her psychological ableness which will mark Ní Chonchúir as a writer of significance.' Rachel J. Fenton, *Melusine*

'...lovely, heartfelt and completely engrossing... *You* might be a short and simple story, but it's evocative – of time, of place, of childhood – and incredibly poignant. I loved every word.' Kim Forrester, *Reading Matters*

'*You* breaks through the traditionalist stained-glass ceiling with a refreshingly modern and urban splintering and scattering of shards. It emerges in the 21st century, intact and with a new way of writing, of *seeing*, which at once heralds the novel as a focal piece of contemporary literature.' Jessica Maybury, *Decomp*

Praise for *Mother America*

'...Ní Chonchúir, like Frida Kahlo, documents female lives in ripe, uncompromising detail. I was also reminded of Edna O'Brien to whose groundbreaking work most Irish women writers owe a debt. Ní Chonchúir's precisely made but deliciously sensual stories mark her as a carrier of the flame.' Cathy Dillon, *The Irish Times*

'...the prose is measured and graceful, rich with delectable turns of phrase and vivid descriptions that seem to paralyse time...Over the past decade, Miss Ní Chonchúir has proven herself a prolific and diverse talent.' Billy O'Callaghan, *The Irish Examiner*

'...Ní Chonchúir...immediately arrests the reader's attention with jolting declarations, oddities and intriguingly out-of-place ideas...A short, satisfying read, *Mother America* offers shards of humour and solace in a collection primarily concerned with the complexities of love...in the difficult task of writing about sex, the author shows particular flair.' Eithne Shortall, *The Sunday Times*

'*Mother America* is a collection that deserves attention and praise not only for its author's mastery of her craft, but also for its poignant language and complexity of human bonding. Reliability lies in the dichotomy between darkness and light, or revelation and obscurity that Woolf so well identified in short story language – and which is a major source of strength for Nuala Ní Chonchúir.' Viviane Carvalho da Annunciação, *The Brazilian Journal of Irish Studies*

'Ní Chonchúir's bravery in forcing her reader to plunge directly into dark waters of the unexpected, the taboo and the downright ugly aspects of motherhood and family, combined with the powerful intimacy of her prose, make hers a literary voice which should and will be heard.' Susan Haigh, *The Short Review*

'...honest, uncompromising, thought-provoking and at times uncomfortable, particularly for the male reader: the [stories] may strike close to home. Each has a point, and makes it. The focus is on mothers but what each reader takes away will vary...Having finished, I put the book down on my bedside table, contemplated it, then started again from the beginning. I challenge you not to do the same.' Dave Troman, *Orbis*

'Towards the end, 'Moongazer', in two pages, took me by the heart and shook me. When I read 'From Jesus to The Moon' I knew I would have to read more of Nuala Ní Chonchúir. Seek her out and see what she sees.' Liam Murphy, *The Munster Express*

THE CLOSET OF SAVAGE
MEMENTOS

THE CLOSET OF
SAVAGE
Mementos

NUALA NÍ CHONCHÚIR

NEW ISLAND

THE CLOSET OF SAVAGE MEMENTOS
First published 2014
by New Island
2 Brookside
Dundrum Road
Dublin 14

www.newisland.ie

PRINT ISBN: 978-1-84840-336-9
EPUB ISBN: 978-1-84840-337-6
MOBI ISBN: 978-1-84840-338-3

Typeset by JVR Creative India
Cover design by Nina Lyons.
Printed by OPOLGRAF SA, Poland

10 9 8 7 6 5 4 3 2 1

New Island received financial assistance from
The Arts Council (An Comhairle Ealaíon), Dublin, Ireland

For Red Tui
&
for Cúan

'Your heart, that place
you don't even think of cleaning out.
That closet stuffed with savage mementos.'
Louise Erdrich, 'Advice to Myself'

Acknowledgments

Thank you to Galway County Council Arts Office for an Artist's Bursary which enabled me to travel to Scotland, and for the residency at the Tyrone Guthrie Centre where some of this novel was written. Thanks to Eoin Purcell for valuable editorial feedback and friendship, and all at New Island - especially Mariel, Justin and Hannah - for doing what they do so well. Big thanks to Deirdre O'Neill, editor extraordinaire, and to Gráinne Killeen for getting the book into readers' minds. Thank you to Nina Lyons for the great cover. A heartfelt miigwetch to Louise Erdrich for letting me adapt a line from her wonderful poem 'Advice to Myself' as the novel's title and for the use of the quote as an epigraph to the book. Thanks, as always, to Finbar McLoughlin and John Dillon for moral and practical support, and so much more besides.

BOOK ONE: 1991

Chapter One

In the church on Ardmair Street, the Blessed Virgin has a Western European face – she is chubby and big jawed. Her form is so familiar to me that I feel comforted and safe, as if I am in the company of an old friend. There is a pink carnation threaded through her fingers, its head is lopped and barely clinging to the stem; the flower is forlorn looking and, to cheer up the statue, I want to pluck it from her hands and replace it with a whole blossom. I have come to pray for Dónal; he is soaking my dreams and I feel close to him all day afterwards, as if he is at my shoulder. He turned up again last night; he stood across my bedroom from me, not saying anything. I watched him and waited for him to speak. I said 'Hiya Dó', but he remained silent.

The statue's robes are made of real fabric – a spangly gown topped with a teal velvet cloak – and tears bubble on her cheeks. She has a halo of light bulbs and one of them is unlit. The prie-dieu digs into my knees and I lean forward, trying to get some relief. I like the sweet, resinous smell in this tiny church; it is different to the incense that lingers in the parish church at home. Here there is only one Mass a week, for the few Catholics who live in the village. I bow my head, close my eyes and search my mind for a prayer. I stopped calling for godly help years ago but, since Dónal's death, the need to pray has crept back in. If God exists, I imagine that He is considering my prayers wryly, the sinner looking for succour when it suits her. But I pray anyway: for Dónal, for my mother Verity, my brother Robin, and for myself. As my Granny King liked to say, praying certainly can't do any harm.

I wonder for a moment if Dónal can hear me, then I dismiss the thought. He hated the church and all about it. He would laugh at me now for being a hypocrite, for being soft. I look up at a squinting portrait of Christ – he looks sceptical in it, as if he is debating something strange that someone has said. Turning back to Mary, I bring my hands up in front of my face; I can feel tears heating the back of my eyes. I push them away and breathe deeply. The statue looks robustly healthy, like a country nurse; she hasn't got the lissom form of Our Lady of Knock. I wonder if she might be the Virgin of Scotland.

'Help me,' I say, not realising I have said the words aloud until a man who is kneeling at the altar hurls a vicious stare in my direction. He stands, genuflects three times, blesses himself over and over, then leaves the church, tossing angry looks at me. I get up, rub at my knees and walk under the stained-glass windows that scatter cheery yellows and blues in my path. I go outside into the welcome saline air and trot the length of Ardmair Street, back to my room in the staff house.

I lie down on the bed to think about Dónal. Missing him is a dull, never-ending buzz in my brain, even six months on. I can't let him in during my day-to-day, but I have to bring him back to me at times. I love the nights when he turns up in my dreams, but think-dreaming him in the daytime – conjuring him up – lets me take him back from death for a while.

Dónal's mother came over to me in the hotel after the graveyard, to thank me again for putting together a memorial board of photographs for the church.

'You did a great job, Lillis; everyone's saying so. Didn't she, Robin?'

'She did,' said Robin, putting his arm around me.

'He looks so good in those photos you took,' Mrs Spain said, 'so like himself. He was mad about the two of you. Always.' She shook her head, still afraid to open her mind to the fact of the accident; to realise that Dónal was gone.

'We were mad about him too, Mrs Spain,' I said, and she nodded. It was hard to look at her and I wished she would go away, back to where her husband was sitting with his limp, empty face.

'I'll go over to Daddy. He's not in the best at all. Devastated.' She nodded and gave me a tight hug. 'You're a smashing girl, Lillis. Give my love to Verity.'

'She was at the church this morning,' I said, but I knew my mother had slipped away after the Mass. She always said that graveyards made her feel guilty for being alive. Mrs Spain squeezed Robin's arm, forced a smile and then she was gone.

Me and Dónal, collecting snowberries in October, tramping around inside the bush in black wellies, filling the scooped-up fronts of our jumpers with the fat, white globes. We throw a few at each other's heads, then snap the rest between our fingers – pop, splat – until our hands are sticky with their pulpy insides.

Me and Dónal, playing with the heavy cushions we have pulled off his mother's sofa. We heft a cushion each onto our backs and pretend to deliver coal to Mrs Spain in her kitchen, in exchange for biscuits, or bread dappled with sugar; she always plays along. The cushions smell like sour apples and farts.

Me and Dónal, stripping the brambles of blackberries, putting as many into our mouths as into the bowl, decorating our faces with their mulched juice. Verity screeches at us when we surprise her with purple-painted faces. Me annoyed with her for being annoyed with us.

Me and Dónal, visiting our elderly neighbour Miss Salmon, to see what goodies we can get out of her. We listen to her girlhood stories of fêtes and dances, charming men and carnivals. Swizzing back the lemonade she gives us, we throw each other looks over the rims of the dusty glasses, and leave Miss Salmon's cold parlour as quickly as we are able.

Me and Dónal and Robin, jumping in and out of the edge of the river, with bellies full of egg-and-cress sandwiches and diluted orange. Both sets of parents drinking beer and smoking on the riverbank, looking young and happy. The boys throwing a beach ball over my head in the water, making me the endless piggy-in-the-middle, until I cry. 'Sissy', they say and 'Sap' and 'Girl', as if being a girl is the worst possible thing. Mr Spain chases them and takes the beach ball away. Me sitting on a picnic blanket close to Verity, listening to the adults' coded talk about The Big C and how much the Spains sold a car for, until my mother shoos me away like a wasp.

Dónal and Robin, pissing in high yellow arcs over my head and giggling madly, then shaking their willies in front of me to get rid of the last few drops. Them making me feel bad because I have to squat to pee; me wetting my knickers, because I need to do it quickly, so they won't catch me there in the bilberry bushes. Me miles behind them when they run off to explore the riverbank, my calves scraped by the low branches of each bush.

Me and Robin, sitting on Dónal and thumping his arms, his face red with fury, until he can wriggle away from us and run home. Him calling back to us, 'You're a pair of bastards', from a safe distance up the lane. The three of us back together again later the same day, hunched on the ground concocting plots and plans, schemes and adventures, soaking hand-drawn maps in tea. Later, we set fire to leaves and twigs with stolen matches, hoping for a blaze.

Me and Dónal, racing our bikes over gravel and skidding hugely, then we compare the marks in the churned-up stones. We cycle to his granny's house in the next village, swallowing the diesel fumes from the buses and lorries on the main road. Cosy at Granny Spain's table, eating shop-bought cake drowned in pink icing, with the sweetest of jam sponging the halves together. Me warily watching Granda Spain who sits by the fire, dribbling onto his shirt like an overgrown baby.

Dónal lying on the grass after a fall into a stand of nettles, crying quietly, his legs a honeycomb of red and white welts. Me rubbing at them with a dock leaf that leaves a snot-coloured trail on his skin. Robin standing over the two of us. 'I never pushed him,' he says. Me giving him a look; an I-know-all-about-you look.

Me and Dónal, sucking on fag butts together, choking and smelly-mouthed, pretending to enjoy them. Robin inhales noisily and blows the smoke into our faces. Me ratting to Verity that Robin smokes. Both grounded for a week and Robin taking it out on me with sly digs and pokes that leave bruises like ever-changing tattoos.

Dónal and Robin, down the back field on a damp afternoon, swigging cans of lager culled from Verity's stash; they topple and laugh, sing and talk gibberish. Soon, lavish vomiting all over the grass. More laughter. Me keeping my distance, hugging my anorak around me, the tip of my nose cold and drippy.

Dónal and Robin, posing for my camera: preens and primps, frowns and grins. Robin, prancing like a pop star; he puckers his lips and minces. Dónal, hazel eyes merry under a crown of red hair, his face a smiling moon. Me enjoying my first shot at portraiture.

Dónal who loves a lake of parsley sauce to go with bacon; who calls socks 'stocks'; who doesn't read books. Dónal who talks about his big brother Cormac like he is a god.

Me and Dónal, walking home from the school disco through the dark, his arm sneaking around me when we stop outside his house. His hands grip my elbows and he rushes a kiss: dry, hard and passionless. He runs inside and slams the door. Me awake all night, running my fingers over his imprint on my mouth.

Dónal working. Me still in school. Him swaggering with the big boys in the village, smoking and spitting, slagging and cursing, calling out to girls. Me stopping to say hi and him looking right past me. Sniggers from his new friends send me skeetering away, hot cheeked and hollow.

Dónal lobbing stones at my bedroom window until I open it, him shouting 'I'm sorry, Lillis' over and over, waving a flagon of cider in one hand and a bag of chips in the other. Me saying, 'Shush, will you?' and laughing. 'Go home, you dope.'

Dónal in my bedsit, me under him. The wet from our sex seeping beneath me. Him begging, 'Be my girlfriend or I don't know what I'll do.' Me saying, 'Stop hassling me, Dónal.' Some of my last words to him.

Dónal, manly in leather, head snugly helmeted, speeding on his motorbike on an icy New Year's Eve, smashing into a wall. Dónal, the photogenic. Dónal, the energetic. Dónal, the funny, the silly, the adventurous, the clever. Dónal, my first love. Lovely, gone-away Dónal.

There is a loud knock on my door and someone calls my name. I pull away from Dónal, roll off the bed and open the door; Struan, my boss, stands there.

'Hi, Lillis. I know you weren't to start until tomorrow officially, but we're short of staff in the bistro tonight. Any chance you'd come over and dig in?'

'I'll get changed and be there in ten minutes.'

'You're a life saver,' Struan says, and claps his hands. 'Excellent.'

He walks down the corridor, shout-singing 'Everything I do, I do it for you.' Struan Torrance is the way I thought he would be but older; he is a lean fifty-something, nearly bald, full of chat and energy. In his advertisement he called himself 'an artisan hotelier', which made me think his place might be interesting even if he sounded like a bit of an eejit. The Strathcorry Inn is more of a lodge than a hotel and there is a smoky, den-like feel to it. Odd artefacts, like fossils and geodes, sit on rickety antique furniture all around the hotel. It has a small art gallery. Verity would love it.

I go through the reception area to get to the bistro and Struan is at the desk; he jumps out of his chair, waving an envelope.

'Lillis, this came for you, I'm so sorry, I forgot; it's a telegram.'

'A telegram?' I grab it and tear it open: *Happy 21st, sweetheart, love Verity*, I read. 'Oh Jesus,' I say.

'Not bad news, I hope?'

'No, no.' I laugh. 'My mother is such a drama queen – it just says happy birthday.'

'Is today your birthday?'

'It is.'

'Och, well then, happy birthday. We'll have a drink tonight.'

I'm not sure if the 'we' means him and me, or everyone on the staff, or what; I thank him anyway and rush through to the bistro to start work. There are only two of us waiting the tables – me and a Scottish girl called Sam. The head chef, Dulcie, is slow and crabby and all I can do is tip-toe around her bad humour.

'It's my bunions – they're *killing* me,' Dulcie shouts, then laughs and points to a waiting order; I am not sure if I am meant to laugh too.

'Hey, new girl, chop, chop,' she barks, and I hoist the plates and swing through the kitchen doors.

Sam tries to train me as we go. She is patient and officious, but it is so busy that I can only muddle along after her, sweating and nervous. I try to carry a plate on my wrist and one in each hand like Sam shows me, but I am terrified of dropping the lot so I revert to the safety of carrying a pair. I attempt to answer questions about the menu from the diners, but Sam has to rescue me every time. Struan helps us out when we get swamped and the night passes quickly in a fug of burnt fingers, the waft of venison and clanging plates. By the end, my feet feel like someone else's feet and all I want to do is lie down. It is a while since I have waitressed and I had forgotten about the aching, overheated feet and the go-go-go.

When the last guests leave, Sam and I clear the bistro tables and set up for breakfast. Struan comes back in.

'Will we jog down to The Windhorse for a drink or will we stay here? It's Lillis's birthday.'

'Oh, happy birthday,' Sam says. 'What age are you?'

'Twenty-one,' I say.

'Aw, hen, why didn't you say?' asks Struan. 'That's a proper birthday. And it's Midsummer's Night. Twenty-one on the twenty first. That's special, eh?'

He clears the dishes from one of the breakfast tables and tells Sam and me to sit. He goes to the wine locker and takes out champagne; he gets glasses from the bar and pops the bottle.

'These are Martini glasses,' Sam says, wiggling hers by the stem.

'Aye, right enough, Sam, but they're fancy,' Struan says, and he pours. We lift our glasses. 'To Lillis. Happy birthday, wee hen.' He kisses the top of my head and I giggle. I see Sam looking at me; I smile but she doesn't return it. We all drink and Struan pours again.

I am lonely as all fuck. I thought I was lonely when I got here, a few evenings since. The bus rattled up from Inverness and, when it stopped on the pier, I looked at the loch and the hills – everything so still and clamour free – and wondered if I would survive more than a few weeks.

Struan met me off the bus and walked me up to the inn. He introduced me to some of the other staff and they nodded and I smiled, but none of their names have stayed with me. Now I am disgustingly homesick and I am not sure there is any cure for that. I even miss Verity.

I left Dublin airport thinking *Ya-boo-hiss, I don't give a shit if I never see this place again,* but I would do anything to be back by the Liffey now, soaking in its brewery and weed stink. I am looking out the window of my tiny staff bedroom: below there is a street of white houses, and beyond that I can see the edge of the sea loch where the water is the plum colour of veins; I can hear ropes thwacking off boat masts and the wheening of gulls. If I crane further, I can see where the hills huddle over Loch Brack and lead it out to sea. I would go for a walk only I have been around the village three times already and I know there is nothing new to see. I can't seem to lift my hand to anything.

Verity warned me I would be lonely.

'You'll miss home, Lillis – the city, Robin, everything,' she said. She was putting the finishing touches to one of her art works – sewing silver buttons onto a tiny waistcoat – and I was standing over her. 'You'll even miss me.'

'I don't think so, Mother.' She reared her head and looked at me. 'No offence,' I added and hugged her. Her body closed against me like a bird folding itself under its wings. I put my hands into the hair at the nape of her neck the way I always did when I was a kid; I sniffed deep on her patchouli and glue smell.

'Come home if Scotland doesn't agree with you,' she said, 'if it doesn't work out.'

'Why would it not work out?' I said. 'It's a waitressing job, Mam, not a career move. I only want to escape for a while.'

'I'm just saying. You're not yourself yet. Dónal's not long dead and you're not back to normal; you couldn't be. And it's a big deal, anyway, going abroad.' She put her sewing down, pulled her hair into a ponytail and smiled. 'Ah, go and enjoy it,' she said, 'you're young. The young are blessed.'

Yes, I do miss her; I miss our sparring. I miss Robin too. And I miss Dónal something rotten.

12

Chapter Two

Kinlochbrack is a fishing village with a Presto supermarket, a gaggle of craft shops and cafés, and obedient seals that bob in the sea loch for the tourists. There is a Caledonian MacBrayne ferry to take you across Loch Brack and the open sea to the Isles, smaller boats provide pleasure trips, salmon farms clutter up the bay, and the rampant smell of fish hangs over everything. Four pubs sit in front of the harbour wall and a group of frowsy B&Bs vie with each other for business. The village swells in the summer with visitors and seasonal staff from all over the world. Struan opened the Strathcorry Inn five years ago and, he says, it is doing better than he could ever have hoped.

I take my camera out early in the morning to catch sunrise over the loch, hoping for dramatic light. The streets are empty. A vanette pulls up beside the bakery and I see Tom the delivery man hoiking baskets of bread and trays of buns in the door; he waves and I salute him. He has been down to Inverness and back already for the bread and it occurs to me that he must never sleep because he was in The Windhorse until midnight with the rest of us. A few herring fishermen in orange waders heap their nets on the pier and call to each other; their laughter lilts like music across to where I sit on the harbour wall, waiting for the sun. I watch them load their gear and smoke cigarettes before chugging out to sea, unzipping the water with their boat.

The loch is flat calm and the navy humps of the hills opposite are like whales, huge and motionless; the air is sea-reeky and cool. When the sun finally pushes up from the horizon it is hidden because of a bank of cloud, but the sky changes from slate to a watery grey. A dazzling line of white appears at the top of the cloudbank. The clouds move up and the sun appears, orange-shimmery, huge and rising fast. I snap and snap, standing on the harbour wall then jumping off it to move up and down Shore Street, looking for the best angles. The sun is a broken wavering blob and I hope some of the weird effects will come through in my photos. The sky turns from salmon to deep yellow and, too soon, to an ashy white. I put the lens cap back on the camera, feeling that disappointment that always settles over me in the aftermath of a beautiful sunrise; the grey morning is, by then, always too grey. But the shots will be good, I think.

Cold has seeped into every part of me so I go up to the inn. I sit in the staff hut that squats in the yard behind the kitchen, to read and drink tea before my shift starts. The Superser, which is always on, burbles in the corner like a contented animal; I enjoy its queasy heat and flickering blue flame. Struan comes in, balancing a scone on top of a mug, a cigarette in his other hand. He sits opposite me and grins like he has something he wants to say, but he pulls on his cigarette and doesn't speak. I look up from my book.

'Yes, Struan? I'm waiting. You look like you're going to explode.'

'I've just realised what it is that your hair reminds me of,' he says, waggling his cigarette, before taking a long drag. 'I have been trying to figure it out for weeks. It's Medusa.' He blows the smoke sideways.

'Medusa? With the snake hair? Wow, thanks.' I look at Struan and he laughs. 'No, really, I'm flattered. What girl doesn't want that comparison made?'

'You've a fine head of hair, Lillis: all those tumbling waves, snaking out from your head.'

'Well, Struan, all I can say in reply is that you have a fine head of skin.'

'You cheeky Irish wench.' He throws a piece of scone across the table and it lands on my book. 'Do you know the Rubens painting *Head of Medusa*?'

'We studied that in art; it's fairly grim. Are you saying I look like her?'

The hut door swings wide and Sam troops in. She is a closed-off girl, I have discovered, superior and watchful. I haven't had to work with her much but, when I do, she is mostly silent. I had thought that we might become friendly but I can see she doesn't want that.

'Is this a private convo or can anyone join in?' she says, sitting beside Struan and looking up into his face; she bites into a piece of toast and talks through it. 'How are you finding the work, Lillian? Feet still sore?'

'Her name is Lil*lis*, Sam. I think you've been told that about a hundred times already,' Struan says.

'Lillis, Lillis,' Sam says, testing my name in a bored way. 'Is that French?'

'Greek,' I say.

'Greek indeed,' Struan says. 'Go on, Medusa, you have cutlery to polish and breakfasts to serve. Get thee to the bistro.'

'Yes, off you go,' Sam says, lighting a cigarette and staring at me. She sucks a froth of smoke up her nose then blows it out through her lips.

'I'm gone,' I say, getting up and squeezing past Sam, who has pushed her chair in front of the door.

Struan follows me out. 'Some girl Sam, eh?'

'She can be a bit rude.'

'Complicated love life,' he says, holding open the kitchen door for me.

'My heart bleeds.'

'Now, now, be nice. Hey, do you fancy a drive later? I got my car fixed and I need to take her out for a run. We could head up north, towards the peaks.'

'Sure,' I say, delighted at the idea of a spin; an hour or two away from the village, a chance to see what lies beyond Kinlochbrack. 'Just don't refer to the car as a she anymore and we'll be laughing.'

We park above Loch Lurgainn and sit looking at Stac Pollaidh, a lone mountain with a scooped peak. It squats – a huge, immoveable tent – blood-dark against the white sky.

'Totally gorgeous, isn't it?' Struan says, stretching his body.

'It's red,' I say. 'The same as Uluru.'

'Sandstone.'

I take photos through the windscreen, feeling too lazy and warm to get out of the car into the windy afternoon. The lake below us is black and I watch a line of gulls follow each other like sheep along its shore. Inside the car the air smells earthy, like a greenhouse. Struan takes two dream rings from a paper bag and we eat them in silence; the white icing makes my teeth ache. I pull the sweet, bready halves apart and lick at the baker's cream that is liberally painted on both sides.

'Fucking yum,' I say. I suck the cream off my fingers. 'Look at me, I'm a total mess.'

Struan holds up his sticky hands. 'Me too; like a wain.'

I lick the sweetness from my skin and mop at the wet with a tissue. 'Tell me something interesting, Struan.'

'Em, let me see,' he says, tapping the steering wheel, 'something interesting. Oh, I know: my father had webbed fingers.'

I look at him and laugh. 'Did he really?'

'Honestly.' He stretches out both hands and dips his index finger through the valleys of the fingers on his left hand. 'They were as webbed as any duck's foot.'

'Jesus, that *is* interesting.'

Struan smiles at me. His looks don't make a great first impression, I think, but they soften as you spend time with him. He is porcine, in ways, with his small eyes and almost bald head, but he is definitely one of those men who, the more you look at him, the more attractive he gets.

'You tell me something now, Lillis. Something *entirely* fascinating.' He lights up a cigarette and rolls down the window a crack.

'Oh, God, pressure.' I think for a moment. 'Well, when I'm reading a book, I always notice when I've reached page one hundred. That page number dances up to my eyes but none of the others do.'

'Hmm. That's sort of interesting,' he says. 'Another thing now.'

'Well…what? Oh, I know, the smell of lavender oil makes my throat close up.'

Struan frowns. 'I have one, this is a good one: there are three golf balls on the moon.'

I laugh. 'No way! That's bollox – no way is that true.'

'It *is* true. I read it in the *Reader's Digest*, so it has to be true. Can you imagine the sound they'd make if you hit them?' He swings an imaginary club. 'Phluck, phluck, phluck.'

'I have one now: my mother stuffs dead animals for a living. She's a taxidartist.' I smile and prod him in the belly. 'Is that fascinating enough for you?'

'It is, actually. What kind of animals?' He squints at me, scratching his cheek.

'She'll use anything really. People know about her now, so she's always being offered road kill and dead pets. Though she usually refuses pussycats and Jack Russells because of what she does to them.' I look down at the lake and wonder how cold it would be for a swim; I shiver.

'Why? What does she do to them?'

'She skins and mounts them and dresses them in costumes. She turns them into works of art. Ultimately, she sells them.' I laugh. 'It sounds a bit obscene when I explain it like that.' I look at Struan. 'She was presented with a monkey recently; she gave it a pipe, a pinny and high heels.' I smile. 'People want to see their pets as they were in real life, not morphed into something weird. So she usually says no to pets and general taxidermy work. Verity prefers oddities.'

'I love it. When do I get to meet this artistic genius? Would she sell me a piece for the Strathcorry?'

'I don't know. She might come over to Scotland sometime to visit me; she's often busy with exhibitions and things.' I wave my hand absently.

'Maybe she'd show in the gallery at the inn? Her work sounds great. *She* sounds great.'

'My mother has her moments, believe me.'

'So much for me and my web-handed dad. He was a bus driver who rarely spoke. I think he thought speech was a kind of affectation. What does your father do?'

'University lecturer; Marine Science. My parents are separated.'

'My mum was a tea lady. The glamour.' He flicks ash out the window. 'Now she's half mad.'

17

'In fairness, your folks were probably a lot better at being parents than mine ever were.'

'Maybe. No, I doubt it.'

Struan stabs his cigarette butt into the ash-tray. He turns to look at me, leans across and gathers handfuls of my hair. He lifts it to his mouth and nose and sniffs.

'What are you doing?'

'I fancy you, Lillis.' He leans over and puts his mouth to mine. His lips are firm but soft and we kiss slowly. He pulls away. 'I've been wanting to do that for weeks.'

'Me too.' We both giggle and he puts his head on my shoulder; I stroke his neck.

'I love your voice, your accent. It comforts me. My mother had an Irish friend when I was a boy; I can't remember her name – it might have been Maura, something like that. Nora, maybe. She was exotic, like a woman from a film. Her nails were always pink, like the inside of a shell, you know? Listening to you talk reminds me of her.'

I move my shoulder so that he has to lift his head and I take his cheeks in my hands; I kiss him. 'Glad to be of service.'

Struan pecks me on the lips, laughs and starts the engine. 'We'd better start moving so we're back in time for the evening shift. We don't want our Lady Sam in a sulk.'

We are quiet on the return drive; the road is narrow and Struan drives fast, swerving into the passing places when other cars approach. The road winds and dips through valleys of rock where sheep teeter, chewing contemplatively. He takes hairpin bends like a rally driver and I cling to my seat. The mountains rise and fall with the meander of the road, sometimes looming hugely, other times seeming smaller, less domineering. Struan names them for me: Bein an Eoin, Cul Beag, Cona Mheall. I spot Highland cows here and there, their faces stuck downwards in never-ending grazing; bog cotton sways festively in dark ditches full of water. I can taste Struan on my tongue and I glance sideways at him while he drives. My mother would approve of him, I think; she is a sucker for a confident man.

18

Verity is on my mind – Robin has written to say that she is drinking too much again and he is worried about her. This is the never-ending story of our mother, the binge-and-rest pattern of her life. Part of me doesn't want to know and part of me needs to keep one eye open to her peaks and troughs.

Back in Dublin, I worked part time in a camera shop. Verity came to see me there one of the last days before I left for Scotland. Even without studying the dough-puffed skin of her face, I knew she had drink on her. Walking from the door to the till, Verity slapped her toes to the floor with aggravated care. Her head was thrown back to give the illusion of control; she stopped when she got to the desk and gripped the counter. I looked at her mouth – set tight like a turtle's – and her squinched up eyes. It had been a quiet day; the shop floor was empty. The air was heavy with the smell of technology and warm from the display lights. I waited.

'I've been thinking,' Verity said, swinging on her feet, 'you should have a baby. That would sort you out.'

'Sort me out?'

'You wouldn't need to go running off to some poxy village in the Scottish Highlands. Why do you need to go there anyway?'

'I like tartan, Mam.'

'You like tartan? God almighty. Be serious, Lillis.' She swiped at her mouth, dragging her lips sideways.

'You're drunk, Mother'

'I had a glass of wine with my lunch,' she said slowly, looking past me; her head bobbed.

'It's four o'clock – it must've been a long, late lunch.'

'Anyway, I want to be a grandmother. All my friends have little ones to fuss over. Tiny doteens to dress up and take around in prams. I have no one, no babies to mind, and it doesn't look like Robin is ever going to get married, so you…' Verity seemed to lose her words; she let her face collapse, then looked at me. 'I'm tired, Lillis. Take me home, sweetheart.'

'I'm working.'

'Lil.' My mother put out her hand: it was big, vein-roped, useless. 'Please, I need to go home.' The small, pathetic voice she used made me move. I told her to sit while I locked up the shop. Verity waited in silence, not speaking again until she was hunched in the back seat of a taxi, oozing the sweet-sick smell of alcohol.

'I hate Mary Cantwell,' she said.

We pulled up in front of my childhood home and stopped. 'How many grandkids has Mrs Cantwell got now?'

'Seven.'

Chapter Three

I watched the quivering lights reflected on the river Liffey while I waited for Robin. We always met on Grattan Bridge – near his flat and my bus stop – and I draped over its low railing, looking at the liver-dark water and the pale, sensuous curve of the Ha'penny Bridge. Even in the dusk light I could make out Robin's loping form on the quay as he came towards me: he swanked when he walked, just like Verity. He lolloped onto the bridge – a TV cowboy – and performed for me: pelvis jutted out, hand on his hip. I laughed, went forward to meet him and gave him a hug.

'How are you? Looking good, anyway,' I said.

He held me away from him. 'You look good too. For a hippy.'

We walked arm-in-arm along the quay towards The Bachelor Inn for our first drink. Town was busy though it was still early. A coven of women, dressed in matching pink tops, burst out of Liffey Street and ran up the Ha'penny Bridge, screeching. I kept pace with Robin's long stride and sucked in the exhaust and river stench of the city. In the pub, Robin sat with his back to the wall and I took the high stool opposite him; he winked at the bar girl who took our drinks order.

'Don't be giving her false hope,' I said, and Robin stuck out his tongue. 'Rob, I went home the other day, to see Verity.'

'Oh?' He fiddled with his shirt buttons.

'Look at you, you have no interest. She keeps saying how much she would love to see you, and that you never ring her, and she might as well not have a son at all.'

'Stop trying to make me feel guilty.' Robin flapped his cigarette box at my face.

'Go and see her. You're her golden boy; she might listen if you say she has to sort herself out, once and for all.'

'Maybe.' Robin bent towards me. 'Hey, do you remember the time you broke her china jug and the two of us buried it in the bottom of the garden? I was thinking about that yesterday.'

'Don't change the subject. And anyway, it wasn't me who smashed it, it was you.' I leaned across and thumped his arm.

'It was *not*. You sent it flying off the table; I remember it well.'

'God, I'd kind of forgotten about that day. She kept at us and at us until we showed her where we'd hidden the bits.'

'Then she locked us under the stairs. Good old Verity and her brilliant parenting.' Robin sipped his drink and looked around the pub.

'I thought Anthony was going to kill her when he found us locked in there. Do you remember the way he shook her? She was pissed, of course, but the way he rattled her, I was sure her head was going to fall off. I thought he was furious with us too.'

'Verity was always fucking mad when you think about it. It's no wonder we're both nuts,' Robin said.

'Speak for yourself, I'm perfectly sane. She was loopers, all right. Still is.' I looked over my shoulder. 'Why do you keep looking past me when I talk? It's driving me mad. Are you expecting someone?'

'No, Little Miss Narky, I'm looking for talent.'

'Seen any?'

'No. What were we saying?'

'About Verity being a crap mother. And a lush.'

'Aw, poor Mumsy.'

'Poor Mumsy, my hole. She's a fucking consequence. You never go near her, so you don't have to deal with it.' I took a long swallow of beer. 'I've gone to her house and found her passed out on the floor twice already this year. She's going to end up dead.'

'With any luck.' Robin wiggled the ice in the bottom of his glass, then took a slug. 'I need to get out of here. I'm thinking San Francisco. Where all the girls wear flowers in their hair. And the boys too, hopefully.'

'San Francisco? What? Where did that come from?'

22

'I've always wanted to go there.'

'First I heard of it. Why?'

'Oh, Lillis, cop on.' He leaned in and ruffled up my hair. 'It's a carnal carnival, man.'

'Jaysus, keep talking like that and you'll fit right in. But please don't come home with some kind of County America accent. That would kill me altogether.'

'Shut up. You're just pissed off because you'll be stuck here forever.' Robin flipped open his lighter.

'I won't, you know. I've got a summer job lined up in Scotland.' I put down my glass.

'You sneaky bitch. How did you get that? We can't both go away.'

'Look, at the moment I *need* your help with Verity. Promise me you'll go to the house and talk to her. We can head out together.'

'Lord, you're so bossy. Is that why you arranged to meet me, to bully me into being our mother's saviour?'

'Rob, just say you'll come with me.'

He held up the palm of one hand. 'OK, OK, OK. I'm feeling positive, anything is possible. Right, it is official: 1991 will be the year Verity finally stays on the wagon. And I'm going to be the one to heave, throw or shove her onto it. I'll be Golden Boy ever more and, for once, it'll be for something I've actually done. Yippee.' Robin clinked his glass against mine and knocked back his drink.

All of the curtains were drawn, giving the house a sleepy, dishevelled look. Robin tapped elaborately on the front door with the Claddagh-ring brass knocker: two arms cradling a crowned heart. I could hear Maxine growling behind the door in her low, yelping way. Opening the letterbox, I curved my finger through and found the string with the key that had hung inside the door since we were kids.

'Hello Maxine, hello girl,' I said to the dog, and she stopped whining.

Robin followed me in; the hall smelt stale, like an empty biscuit tin. Maxine couldn't lift her fat body to greet us; she looked up from her blanket and thumped her tail. She is past it, I thought, looking at her grey muzzle and old-age spread. The whole house was quiet and dark.

'Verity,' Robin called; there was no reply.

We went through the sitting room to the kitchen; a cobweb like the sail of a yacht hung from the ceiling over the table. The cobweb wavered as I walked past it to survey the counter, which was a jumble of caked dishes and pots.

'Jesus, look at this. How does it get so bad so quickly? I was here only last week.'

'Limerick lace, that's what they call that.' Robin pulled the cobweb down and rolled it into a clump.

'The table's a mess.' There was a bowl with rancid butter; hillocks of breadcrumbs; filthy knives and spoons; and plate upon plate with congealed gloops of food.

'This is squalor,' Robin said, 'true, honest-to-God squalor.'

The kitchen smelt exactly like my Granny King's had, even though Granny's was always pristine; the smell was sugary like a baker's shop. My granny used to say, 'You could eat your dinner off my floor.' As a child I was never able to answer that because I couldn't figure out what kind of person would want to eat their meat and potatoes off lino.

I followed Robin back out to the hall; he was peering up into the stairwell.

'Mam,' he called. 'Verity!' He looked at me and shrugged. 'We'd better go up,' he said.

We trundled up the stairs to Verity's bedroom but she wasn't there; we came back down and went into her studio. The trappings of her art lay in awkward piles on the bench and on the floor: rolls of chicken wire, bags of plaster, boxes of glass eyes, her cutters. A half-mounted goat showed its open hindquarters to the room. I looked at the clatter of empty bottles on the floor and saw our mother on the chaise longue by the far wall, curled up and shivering.

'Mam,' I called, the word emerging on a wail as I went towards her.

'For fuck's sake, Verity,' Robin said, pulling a throw over her and moving the bottles.

'Anthony?' she said, thinking he was our father; she managed to sound querulous, even in a whisper.

'Anthony's long gone, Mother,' he said, 'it's me, Robin. Lillis is here too.'

'Aw, Rob,' she said, in a childish voice, 'thank God it's you; I don't want that fucker of a husband of mine anywhere near me.'

I came into the ward and walked past half a dozen sleeping old women until I found her.

'Did you bring my good nightdress?' Verity was propped up in the bed, wearing a hospital gown. I looked at her loose hair and the skin pouched under her chin in flaps. She looks ragged, I thought.

'Yes, the nightie is in here,' I said, handing over a plastic bag. 'What did they say?' I asked Robin.

'The usual. She was dehydrated, she has to stop drinking, her foot's in danger of falling off…'

'What?' Verity said.

'Only joking,' Robin said. 'Just making sure you're *compos mentis*, Mother, that's all.'

'I'm not going back into John of God's, so you needn't even think it,' Verity said, pointing at us. 'It's a fucking nut-house, full of mad fools. I can't stand the place.'

'Keep your voice down,' I said.

'No, I won't keep my voice down, young lady, and don't tell me to. I'm not going back there, I'm going home.'

'Whatever you say, Verity,' Robin said, yawning.

'And you needn't tell your father I'm in here. The last thing I want is him foostering about, giving orders and treating me like a child.'

'He already knows you're in hospital,' I said.

'Well, thank you, Lillis, thank you for that.'

'It wasn't Lil who told him, it was me. He likes to know how you are, so I rang him with the latest,' Robin said.

Verity harrumphed. 'Can't he ring *me* if he wants to know how I am? Too busy making a fool of himself with that child he's with. The darkie.'

'Mam, stop.'

'What? Don't come over all holier-than-thou with me, Robin Yourell. She's black and their brats are half-caste and that's telling it like it is.' Verity cackled. 'Making a bloody eejit of himself having more kids at his age.'

I tutted. 'You get worse by the minute, do you know that? You're like some crackpot hag spitting bile. I don't know why I expected anything else from you. India is from, guess where? *India*. Via Manchester or some bloody place.'

'Oh, shut up, Lillis. Nobody wants to hear you. You've been a whiner since the day you were born. Whingy, nervy, needy Lillis.'

'Right, that's it.' I grabbed my bag and stood up.

'What are we going to do with you, Mother?' Robin said, looking from her to me.

'Let Lillis go off in a huff, if that's what she wants. It gets her out of my face. She's an almighty nag.'

'She only nags because she cares. You're wearing her out, Mam.'

'I'm actually still here you know,' I said.

'I don't ask Lillis to come and visit me – she just turns up. All I want is to be left alone.' She pulled Robin's arm, shook it hard and shouted. 'Why don't the pair of you just fuck off and leave me alone?'

Robin's flat was tucked in the basement of a tenement off Capel Street. I sat in a hard-armed chair and watched him make coffee in the kitchenette.

'I don't know how you can you live here. Apart from the grime, my knees are nearly in the next room. I feel all closed in, like I'm sitting on a bus.'

Robin swivelled his hip to avoid the counter's edge and swung back the opposite way quickly, so as not to knock into the door to the bathroom. He sat down and handed me a mug; I wiped the rim with my sleeve before taking a sip.

'I washed that cup.'

'Everything about this place is disgusting: it's a pigsty, a rat-hole.'

'Thank you for the wonderful animal comparisons, Lillis; personally I like to think of the place as Robin's Little Nest.' He grinned. 'Anyway, I won't be here much longer: San Fran beckons, after all.' He gulped his coffee. 'I went home to visit Verity yesterday.'

'Oh yeah?' I looked at him.

'They let her leave the hospital on the condition that she stays dry and goes for counselling once a week. AA too, if she can manage it.'

'She won't do AA after the last time.'

'Verity says that the binge was "brought on" by Bronagh at the gallery. Bronagh hinted that it was getting harder to sell her pieces. She made the mistake of telling Verity she needs to start painting again.'

'I'd say that went down well.'

'Apart from the fact that she hates being told what to do, she says she doesn't want to paint. But, apparently, stuffed animals are a tough sell these days. They're not PC, so it doesn't matter how arty-farty or beautiful they look.' Robin scratched his head. 'She was wondering aloud when you might be over to see her.'

'Was she really, now? And will I be abused and screeched at from the minute I walk through the door, do you think?'

'Of course you will, she can't help herself. Ah no, she's feeling sorry for what she said to you at the hospital and even sorrier for her vodka-free self. Will you go?'

I pulled a face at him. 'I suppose.'

'I'll go with you. Moral support and all that.'

Verity had made a Sunday dinner and the house felt fresher than it had in a long time. The sun threw strands of lemon light across the kitchen, heating up the whole room and reminding me of other Sundays. Robin rattled a greeting at Verity and I sat straight down at the table.

'Don't I even get a hello?' Verity said.

'Hi.'

'I see, we're in monosyllabic mode, are we?' Verity said, turning back to the stove to thrash at a pot of potatoes with a masher.

'Now, now, Mam, be nice.' Robin grabbed our mother around the waist and kissed her cheek; she smiled at him and began ladling the dinner onto plates. We ate in silence for a while, the food and the sun's rays warming us.

'This is lovely,' I said, 'thanks.'

'You're welcome,' Verity said, chewing slowly on a small piece of steak, not looking at me. The light from the window was streeling across her face; I looked at the shirred skin around my mother's eyes and realised she was starting to look her age.

'Have you heard?' I said. 'Golden Boy is heading for the Golden Gate.' I forked a pile of mash into my mouth and looked at Verity.

'What are you on about?' Verity poked at the gravy-drenched broccoli on her plate and shucked off her cardigan from her shoulders. 'It's abnormally hot in here.' She looked at Robin. 'What's this, Rob? Are you going away somewhere too?'

'Dublin feels small to me these days, that's all; I'm thinking I might go to the States.'

Verity's face clamped up. 'Oh, very nice. Very nice, indeed.' She started to hum a high, pointless tune. 'Everyone is leaving me.'

'You know, more than likely, I won't go at all.' Robin glanced at me, then Verity. She was looking at her plate and hacking at the food, her eyebrows pointed into high peaks.

'I suppose this was your idea,' Verity said, spiking her knife at me.

'For fuck's sake,' I said, throwing down my cutlery. 'What is wrong with you?' I shoved back my chair and stood up.

'Come on, come on.' Robin waved at me to sit down; I stayed on my feet. 'Mam, of course Lillis didn't come up with the idea of me going to San Francisco. Why would you even think that?'

'Give me strength! Because she's jealous of how close you and I are and she always has been. *That's* why.'

'I am not! I amn't.' I hovered over the table staring down at my mother. 'You have got to stop thinking that, Mam, it's not true. If anything, I do my best to bring the two of you closer.' I tossed my napkin on top of my half-eaten dinner.

'Mam, you promised you wouldn't pick a fight today. Now look what you've done.' Robin sat back and frowned. 'Why are you always at Lillis?'

'I'll tell you why: I hate people who remind me of myself. And Lillis reminds me so much of me that I could kill her.' Verity pushed her plate, knocking most of her food onto the table top.

I got up and went into the sitting room; Robin followed. I stood at the window, looking out at a group of kids playing football on the street.

'She doesn't mean it, you know,' he said.

'I wish I could believe that, Rob, but I'm entirely fed up with her at his stage. I'm going to go.' I reached down to the floor and scooped up my bag. 'I remind her of herself. Jesus. There's no hope for me, is there?' I smiled at Robin. 'I think it's time for me to take an *interregnum* from Verity. My only worry is that if I'm not around to be lorded over and bullied, she's sure to start on you. Whatever you do, don't let her guilt trip you into not going away.'

I hugged Robin and told him to give me a ring. I let myself out of the front door. One of the kids called to me and I dropped my bag and kicked ball with them for a few minutes, then went on my way again. I knew that Robin or Verity would be watching from the windows; I waved back at the house, without turning around, and walked on.

Chapter Four

The sand is packed into hard, ridged hillocks on Achmelvich beach; I scuff my toes through it, trying to find a powdery patch to warm my feet. I toss my sandals into a clump of marram grass, fold the back of my skirt under my bum and sit down. The husk of a tyre flaps in the sand near my feet and I wonder how it made it here. The sea is alien to me. I love it, but every time I am by the sea I realise how little I know about it; I crave the extra knowledge that people who grew up beside the ocean have. Turning my nose to the water, I breathe deeply on the seaweed and grass smell. It is quiet where I sit, I am surrounded by silence; every sound, even the breaking waves, seems to come from very far away.

Struan is running with a blue and green kite near the shoreline, trying to get it aloft. It whooshes high for a few seconds, tail ribbons flipping, and I can hear his delighted yelps, but the kite soon spins down to the beach again. He runs to it and tosses it high once more. I watch him make a few more attempts to get it flying before he begins to roll the line – there isn't enough wind.

He waves to me, then beckons hugely, rolling his arm and bowing his body forward like a child. I listen to the sea, a far-off roar, and watch Struan. He points to the sand, and scissor-jumps in mock fear; he is still holding the kite and its tails sally out behind him. He is gorgeously remedial, I think, and grin to myself, but I don't get up – it is nice sitting in the hush of the dunes. But I know Struan won't come to me. He will stay where he is until I go over to him, making a mime show of his movements; he is stubborn like that. There is something he wants me to see and I have to disturb myself to go and partake; that is what he expects. I pick up my sandals and stroll towards him.

'Look,' he says, when I get close, 'just look at this.' There is a wide jellyfish at his feet; it is globular and translucent as sea glass. 'It looks like a big snot,' Struan says and pretends to sneeze onto the sand. 'Ha ha choo.'

'You're so juvenile.' I shake my head and smile. He dances me over the jellyfish. 'Mind my feet, those things sting, you know.' I grab my hand from his and back away from him. 'My God, there's an army of them. Look!' We both stare down the strand towards the sea – there are scores of jellyfish stalking up from the tide line.

'Argh,' Struan shouts, running and staggering, 'help, help, they're trying to kill me.' I wait for him to stop; I catch up, take his hand and we walk.

'I've only seen a jellyfish once before – on holiday in Galway as a kid,' I tell him. 'Verity had bought me a pair of white clogs and they were toe-pinchers. She sent me into the sea in them, saying the saltwater would soften up the leather. When I got into the first waves I saw a brown jellyfish and I ran screaming from the water, losing one clog.' I laugh. 'Verity was furious. My father was delighted, though – he hated those clogs. He said they looked like two loaves of bread on my feet.'

'I'd say you were a spoilt brat when you were a kid, with all the latest of everything. Daddy's little angel.'

'Shut up. I was not.' I dig him in the side.

Struan takes me into his arms and hugs me. 'You're *my* angel.' He kisses my mouth; I close my eyes only when we are both deep into the kiss. When we pull our lips from each other's I hold him hard against me, breast to chest. Fulmars skirl overhead, looking like origami birds sent to put on a stilted air show; they career and drop, holding themselves stiff as paper.

'I should tie the kite to a gull,' Struan says, 'that would get it going.'

'Struan, I might have to go home for a weekend soon. I got a letter from Robin – Verity is not in the best. Again. She's driving him mad.'

'How so?' He holds me with one arm; the kite skitters in his free hand when the breeze catches it.

'Ah, it's the usual. She turned up at his office, half cut, ranting about being lonely and alone. He brought her home, then had to stay with her until she fell asleep.' I sigh. 'She was locked. He thinks she needs to go back into John of God's, but he's having trouble convincing her.'

'And he thinks she'll listen to you?'

'Not necessarily, but Robin wants the backup. We can kind of double-team her.'

'Well, whenever you need to go, just say. You can have a few days' leave, don't worry about it.'

'Thanks. You could come with me, you know.'

'Maybe I will. It's years since I was in Ireland.'

We walk back along the beach to the dunes; I go ahead of Struan up a hump and, in its hollow, I almost fall onto a woman who sits feeding her baby. The full moon of one breast is released from her swimming togs and the baby's red mouth is puckered around the dark areola.

'Oh, I'm sorry,' I say, retreating. I stumble and slide in the sand, then move backwards to fend off Struan, but he is already on top of me.

'Struan Torrance. Hello!' the woman says, squinting up at us.

'Ah, Margaret. Are you well? I heard you were back.'

The baby turns one eye up to survey us and it keeps on suckling. I can't seem to unhook my gaze from the woman and the blue veins that trace like rivers on a map over her breast. Her baby's fat hand kneads the skin around the nipple protectively.

'We're back for good; we bought a house at the end of Market Street. You're our neighbour.'

'That's great. Call in and see me anytime, to the house or the inn. Come up for a drink. Dinner.' Struan stands with his hands on his hips, looking down. 'You're the Madonna of the Dunes, Margaret, sitting there.' He laughs. Margaret laughs too. Struan introduces us; she and her husband have been living in London, she tells me.

'I used to work at the inn,' she says.

'You and everyone else in Kinlochbrack,' I say and, realising I sound a bit cranky, I smile. 'What's the baby's name?'

'This is Charlie.'

'Bonnie Prince Charlie,' Struan says.

Margaret unlatches the baby from her breast by sticking her pinkie between his lips and her nipple; Charlie flails and looks accusingly at us.

'Will you take him a sec?' Margaret thrusts Charlie up at me. I grab him under the armpits and heave him up to my chest. He is wearing only a nappy and his skin is butter soft. He slumps against me and I squeeze his lamb-chubby thighs.

'His fat legs,' I say, 'they're irresistible.' Charlie snuggles his face into my shoulder and the heft of him is beautiful. I don't ever remember holding a baby before. Margaret pulls up the shoulder strap on her togs and stands.

'Now,' she says, taking the baby, and I am surprised that I am reluctant to hand him back. I can't look at her face in case she reads me, so I look down; her toenails are painted a sparkly black.

'Cool nail varnish.' I feel like a teenager as I say it, let loose in the company of adults.

'I think so.' She wiggles her toes. 'I feel cool when I wear it.'

'Hey, if you ever need a babysitter.'

'Wow, thanks so much, Lillis. Me and Gordon haven't been out in ages; I'll probably take you up on that.' She grins.

Struan helps Margaret gather her picnic blanket, towels and basket, and we walk her back to her car. He asks after Gordon.

'Och, he's fine. No accountant is ever out of work. And work makes Gordon happy.'

'We'll see you around Kinlochbrack,' I say.

Margaret stops and hooshes Charlie onto her shoulder; she looks at me. 'Your accent. My mother was from Dublin. She died last year.'

'I'm sorry to hear that,' I say.

Struan puts his hand on Margaret's shoulder and she nods, acknowledging the gesture. She scoops Charlie into his seat and straps him in. We watch them drive away.

'A great girl, Margaret,' Struan says. 'One of the best.'

'Presto has gooseberries,' Dulcie says, her eyes lit up like new love. 'Tom dropped by to tell me. Here, go and get me some.' She hands me a ten pound note.

I slip out of the inn's kitchen by the back door and walk in the sunshine to Shore Street. The place mills with tourists; they are a writhing, smiling sea of leisure. They idle on the footpaths and clog up shop doorways, so that I have to dodge on and off the path, into the slow flow of traffic, to avoid them. But I am glad to see the tourists all the same; they look happy – they make a languid, oozing mass of contentment. A trio of ducks flies frantically up from the harbour, flapping as if afraid they might fall from the air. The tourists shield their eyes to watch, some take photographs, and they all cheer when the ducks make it over the rooftops and out of sight.

Presto has five small trays of gooseberries left. I buy the lot. I drop one into my bedroom in the staff house and take four back to Dulcie in the kitchen. Struan is there, chopping vegetables because the kitchen porter has not shown up.

Dulcie takes the trays from me. 'I'm going to make Gooseberry Fool.'

'Old fool makes new fool,' Struan says.

Dulcie swipes at him and he grabs her into his arms and waltzes around the kitchen, humming Strauss as he goes.

'Let me go, you fucking madman,' Dulcie says, but she beams and submits to the dance.

'Struan, I'll call around to yours later,' I say, and he winks at me over Dulcie's shoulder, then spins her past the sink.

Struan's place is a two-bedroomed fisherman's cottage and it huddles in a row of identical ones on Clanranald Street. I carry my tray of gooseberries to his house, stopping in Presto for a bag of sugar and some scones on the way. Struan spends so much time at the inn that his home is always clean and neat, barely lived-in, which I love. The house seems to wait for us, as patient as an old dog, and it springs to life when we walk its rooms. It smells of tobacco but also of the rosemary oil that Struan sprinkles on the radiators. His furniture is second hand and rough, which makes me feel at home. Verity could never pass a skip without pulling out a chair or a table – it didn't matter how broken up or filthy. I have always liked the way other

34

people's heirlooms shed their history as they settle down in a new owner's rooms.

I lift the hinge of the door knocker and bang it, still not feeling I have the right to use the key Struan gave me, when I know he is inside.

'Well, helloooo,' he says, opening the door.

'Are you trying to sound sexy?' I ask, kissing him.

'Do I *not* sound sexy?'

I hold up the gooseberries and sugar. 'Jam,' I say.

'Contraband. Did you nick those on Dulcie?'

'I bought them. I wanted to make you some jam.'

We sit at the kitchen table together, top and tailing the fruit, listening to the dance music that Struan has recently decided he loves. He boogies in his chair, elbowing me to join in. When the jam is at a rattling boil on the stove, he gets up and goes riffling through the food press.

'We need ginger,' he says, pushing jars and tins to and fro along the shelves. 'Where the fuck is it?'

'We don't need ginger.'

'I thought you said this jam was for me and I like ginger with goosegogs.'

'Oh my God – you're such a whinge-bag sometimes. Here, let me look. And it's goose*gobs* not goose*gogs*.'

'Gobs. Gogs. Who cares?' I find some ground ginger and toss it in; Struan stands over the pot, stirring the jam with a smug smile. 'Domestic bliss,' he says.

Struan carries the jam and scones up the stairs on a tray. I strip, tossing my clothes onto the bedroom chair, and we eat and drink tea, sitting up in Struan's bed.

'The perfect way to spend my afternoon off, I must say.'

'Mmm,' Struan says. 'And thanks. It was very sweet of you to think of making jam. No one has ever done that for me before.'

'Hey, you're welcome. You're always doing stuff for me, dinners and that, so I thought it would be a change.'

He kisses my shoulder and flicks my nipple with one finger. 'It's nice of you.'

'What can I say? I'm a nice girl.' I kiss his nose. 'It's a while since I made jam. Me and my friend Dónal made it as kids. We'd spend hours collecting blackberries, then his mother would let us loose in her kitchen. Mrs Spain had the patience of ten saints. Unlike Verity.'

'You make your mother sound awful. Is she really that bad?'

'Worse.' I lick jam off my fingers, enjoying its tang. 'One time me and Dónal smeared blackberry juice all over our faces and crept into my mother's studio. We shouted "Boo!" and she nearly dropped. She roared at us, nearly killed us – we genuinely scared her. I remember thinking she couldn't take a joke like a normal person, but she thought we'd burnt our faces or something.' I slide my fingers up and down along Struan's arm, feeling the tension of his muscle. 'She was always angry, my mother.'

'Dónal? Is that Irish for Donald?'

'I dunno. Maybe Donald is Scottish for Dónal.' I put my plate and cup on the bedside locker. 'Dónal died last New Year's Eve.'

'Jesus, I'm sorry. That's rough. What happened?'

'Motorbike crash.'

I shift my body and lie on Struan; I pull up his shirt so that my head is on his bare chest.

'I've lost friends along the way. It takes a while to get over,' he says.

I prop my chin on his breastbone and look up at him. 'You're the first person I've been with since him.'

'Were you more than friends then, you and this Dónal?'

I nod. 'We were, you know, friends mostly but sometimes we…' I push tears away and Struan holds me.

'Shush, now, it's OK. It's hard to lose someone, especially suddenly like that.'

I wriggle around and lie with my back along Struan's front. I look at the shoeboxes stacked like coffins along the wall and the shelf opposite the bed that holds a row of Caithness glass. Struan collects paperweights in shades of blue and they are mesmerising when the sun slants through them, as it does now, throwing their colours onto the white wall. My favourite is a deep-blue oval paperweight that seems to suspend the sea in its core; Struan calls it the plumbago egg. Inside it, bubbles of glass rise to the top around golden coral and ferny pink seaweed. To me, it looks like fireworks have gone off underwater.

I was surprised the first time I saw the paperweights. Collecting them seemed a peculiarly feminine passion, but now I see that they are pure Struan: he loves to display beautiful things for the simple sake of beauty. I watch the blue and white swirls of the reflected glass on the wall as Struan's hands glide up my belly to cup my breasts. He kisses my neck and pulls me so that I lie under him; he flips me onto my stomach and kisses my spine from root to tip.

Chapter Five

Sam divvies up the tips; it is Struan's night off. He has gone to Inverness to see a film with Tom the bakery man and Dulcie the chef. They were like three teenagers on a skite as they got into Struan's car, giggling and pucking at each other. Sam plops a pile of one pound notes and a few coins into my hand.

'Riches, huh?' she says. 'Do you want to go for a drink?'

I don't really – not with her. 'Just the one,' I say. 'I'm wrecked.'

Sam shrugs. 'Don't worry; I won't keep you up all night.' She lights a cigarette. 'Want one?'

'I don't smoke.'

We leave the hotel by the side door and walk along Ardmair Street. The moon hangs over the hills by the loch; its milk-light glows like a headlamp onto the water.

'Beautiful moon,' I say, as we dip down towards Shore Street.

'Do you like working at the inn?'

'It's grand.'

'Grand, grand, grand. That's all you ever say.' Sam pulls a comb out of her pocket and rakes it through her hair, with vicious strokes. 'So, you and Struan, eh? When did that happen?'

'I don't know; soon after I got here.'

'He always goes for the new girl,' she says, sucking on her cigarette.

It is a well-aimed dart and it lodges in my stomach, pricking at me. I lift my face to the sky to catch a breeze and watch the moon anchored in the black, ancient and necessary; a cloud drifts then hangs in front of the moon, like a bruise on its skin. Below us, in the harbour, the sea-rusted hulls of boats clank and groan. We trot along in silence.

'How long have you worked in The Strathcorry, Sam?'

'Three years.' She flicks her cigarette butt into the path of an oncoming car. 'I was the new girl once.'

Sam pushes open the door of The Windhorse and I follow her inside. The pub is busy; some of the herring boats are in and the bar is lined with welly-wearing fishermen, all of them in plaid shirts and jeans – the Kinlochbrack uniform. The blood and guts smell off the men makes me want to be back at the staff house, safe in my room, in my bed. Sam walks up to a group and greets each of them by name; unlike herself, she is laughing and chatty and I stand behind her. I watch a couple who sit side by side on one of the banquettes like two magnets repelling each other. The woman lifts her drink to her lips, sips, puts it down. Her husband slurps from his pint, lowers it. They look straight ahead, the distance between them on the seat stretching to miles.

Sam turns away from the fishermen and hands me a pint of lager; her smile drops.

'Relax, Lillis,' she says, 'you're always so wound up.' She points to free seats near the happy couple and I shuffle ahead of her and sit.

'I don't feel wound up,' I say, my shoulders turning to iron as I say the words.

'I've seen you coming out of the church on Ardmair Street,' Sam says. 'Devout, are you?'

'No, I like to go in sometimes, to think.' I swig my pint.

Sam snorts. 'You know you might be better off taking a wee job on the Isle of Barra. That's where all the Catholics are.'

'Hardly *all* of them; there's a small congregation in Kinlochbrack. Struan is a Catholic. Of sorts.'

She looks away even as I speak and lights a cigarette. I watch the door, thinking Struan might make a late drink. I am feeling away from myself after having only half a pint and I am struggling to find even one reason to stay out with Sam. It's clear she doesn't like me and I certainly don't like her. Sam tosses her head and drags on her smoke. Her hair is greasy, something I have noticed about her before, and I'm afraid to breathe too deeply in case I smell its unctuous heat.

'Is it serious?' Sam says, whipping around to stare at me. Her eyes are violet-blue, like Achill marble – the strangest I have ever seen.

'With Struan?' I say. 'Well, I like him. It's early yet.'

'Huh,' she says. 'Watch him, that's all I'd say. He's one of those blokes who always has to have a woman by his side. Always. It's not long since the last one.' She eyeballs the couple nearby; they are still staring ahead, blank faced. 'Look at them: Sadness and Charisma. That will be you and Struan in ten years' time.' She laughs, a dull, short noise that she coughs out of her throat.

I get up and go to the bar; the fishermen clear a space and stay silent while I order another pint for Sam. When I turn away, one of them says something; I miss it but the others snicker.

'That's Struan Torrance's bird,' a voice says.

'Oh, aye? Is she working at the inn? She's bonny.'

I go to the toilet and come back to the bar for Sam's drink; the fishermen are discussing the trial of some locals who were jailed for cocaine smuggling in the harbour. They laugh about the long sentences the men face, but their relief that it is not them is clear.

'Twenty-five years Murdo got.'

'Fuck me.'

'He was always a stupid bastard.'

'He better keep his arse to the wall inside.'

They all laugh. Sam is missing when I get back to our table, so I put down the pint I have bought for her beside her half-full glass and leave.

I am surprised to find a cloak of mizzle over the village when I step outside the pub; the evening had been so clear. This is the Scottish weather I have been waiting for; I am tired of the uncharacteristic sunshine that has lit up the days since I arrived. The moon is a cotton-edged blur above the loch now and the boats bounce in the harbour, knocking against each other like drunken dancers. Tail-lights and headlights retreat and advance through the rain on the streets in blurs of red and white. I hurry back to my room, glad to be away from The Windhorse and Sam.

A high wind beats around the staff house the whole night like huge, whomping wings, making me jerk in and out of sleep. I neither dream nor don't dream – I feel trapped in a waking-sleeping limbo and the wind whirrs in my ears all night, it seems. In the morning I drag myself into the shower and then into my uniform; I let myself out of the staff house. The day is grey; I watch a pink contrail sail across the clouds like a comet as I walk up towards the hotel to start the breakfast shift. I meet Sam, weaving her way down Ardmair Street, towards me; she sits on the low perimeter wall of the staff house and tries to put a match to a cigarette.

'Will I light it for you?'

She looks up at me and hands me the matches. 'You missed the party,' she slurs, barely able to lift her head.

Her collapsed state reminds me of Verity and I want to get away. 'Oh?' I say, setting the match to her cigarette; only one side lights and it takes her a while to drag on it.

'At Struan's. We had the best of laughs.' Sam lurches off the wall and heads towards the staff house; she stops, turns and stabs the air with her finger. 'Your so-called boyfriend's house. Get me?'

Struan doesn't appear in the bistro all morning; we have few guests and I wait the tables on my own, relieved not to be dealing with Sam and her hangover. In the afternoon I go to the pier and take a pleasure boat to the Summer Isles. It is the wrong day to go on a boat trip – the hills around the loch are skeined in mist and we can barely see ten feet in front of us – but it feels good to be out on the water. I rub my hand along the boat rail and my skin comes away dappled with salt. I lick my hand and catch a German tourist examining me; he smiles and turns away. Buoys like outsized tangerines bounce on the water as Kenny, the skipper, brings the boat near rocks to show us fat piebald seals, content as kings, lolling in groups. They remind me of enormous slugs ; they lift their heads then drop them when we idle past, barely interested in us. A few of the smaller seals let contented yelps as if saying hello to us.

'Thousands of seals a year are being shot by salmon farmers,' Kenny announces, over the microphone, and I look at the seals on the rocks, their trust in us and our noisy boat so misplaced. Kenny keeps up a commentary about seabirds, and the minke whales and porpoises that sometimes appear in Annat Bay.

I think over what Sam was saying about Struan; I can brood on it or I can leave it go, I know. It doesn't surprise me that he always has a woman; I didn't imagine he was a bachelor before I turned up. But, at 51, how many women? And what happens to them all? I wonder mostly why Sam wants to tell me this stuff; why she feels the need to dig at me. I watch the spray from small waves lift up in our wake until I am mesmerised, by the churning foam and by my drifting thoughts. I shake myself up and push Sam and her remarks away. It is hard to know what lies further beyond the boat. When we come against a cliff face to look at sea caves, the black rock looms so suddenly out of the mist that some of the passengers gasp, as if a monster has risen from the sea to tower over us.

On the way back to shore, Kenny switches off the Tannoy, and the sun, miraculously, pushes through the mist, lifting it quickly up and over the sea. The flank of Ben Mor Coigach is combed in sunlight and the lighthouse looks as small as a gull beneath it. We shunter past a salmon farm and see the fish leaping in their pens while men in high-vis vests smoke cigarettes and toss feed from buckets. It seems the loneliest of jobs, stuck out on the sea with only the salmon and their stink for company.

I sit on one of the benches along the side of the boat, feeling the engine's thrum deep inside me, and enjoying the clean water smell mixed with the sharp wind. Most of the German tourists have their eyes closed now, soaking up the sun; I look at their ruined legs and swollen ankles bulging over the sides of sensible shoes. The boat moves quickly, but being on it soothes me; I like rocking with the sea's movements, and being cut off from work and from everything else.

Struan is standing on the pier when we dock. He says hi to Kenny and helps me out of the boat. He hands me a punnet of peaches.

'Thanks. How did you know I was on a cruise?'

'Sam told me – she saw you get on the boat.'

'Is that mad bitch following me?'

He puts his arm around my shoulder and we walk up Shore Street. 'You heard about last night.'

'I heard nothing only that you had a party.' I rip the net covering the peaches and hand him one.

'When we got back from Inverness I went to The Windhorse looking for you, but you were gone. I came down and knocked on your window.'

'You could have let yourself in.' I bite into a peach and the juice slews down my chin.

'I didn't want to scare you.'

'Sam was saying things last night. About you and the way you are with women.'

'Don't mind Sam, she's only trying to get your goat.' He rubs at his head.

'She doesn't like me, Struan.'

'She likes you well enough. Sam's a bit contrary, that's all.'

'Well, I don't like her much either, so we're quits. Anyway, what did you get up to last night? And bear in mind, I'm Irish – I don't want brutal honesty. Lie gently, please.'

'There's no need for any lies, Lillis. We fancied a drink after being in Inverness; Tom, Dulcie and a wee crowd from the pub came back to mine. That's all. We had a few beers and I strummed guitar badly.'

'I met Sam rolling home when I was going to work this morning.'

'She fell asleep on the sofa. Sam's a narcoleptic drunk, Lillis. She keels over after three pints.'

'So I've nothing to worry about?'

He stops and flicks his peach stone into the harbour; I throw mine after his. He takes my two wrists in his hands.

'Hey, what would you have to worry about? Come here.'

He kisses the top of my head and I put my arms around his waist and look up into his face. The waterlines of his eyes are red raw. I bury my face in his shirt and breathe on the deodorant and old beer smell. I hear a wolf whistle; I look up to see Kenny passing.

'That one's young enough to be your daughter, Torrance.'

'Fuck off, man,' Struan says, slapping Kenny's shoulder and laughing.

We walk hand in hand to Struan's house on Clanranald Street, me swinging my punnet of peaches like a handbag. The street is empty and hushed. In a display of people's innate love of symmetry, the middle windows of all the houses on Struan's terrace are open, to let the ozone smell of the sea rush through the rooms. Inside his house it feels cool and I rub down the goosebumps that pop out all over my arms.

'I'll light the fire,' Struan says.

'Do you think we need one?'

'Och, it'll be nice,' he says, and disappears out the back to get firelighters and coal.

The fire is a flop: it smokes and its desultory heat seems to set up the evening badly. After a dinner of leftover soup from the Strathcorry's kitchen, we sit on the sofa, listening to music and reading the newspapers. Verity has the same album – something plaintive by Fleetwood Mac – and I am reminded of her, dancing drunkenly to it night after night when my father left; the music niggles at me, it makes me feel maudlin and bad. Struan's eyes are closed and his head droops forward. The paper he has been reading slides from his lap to the floor.

'Do you want to go to bed, Struan? You're falling asleep.'

'I'm resting my eyes.'

I tut. 'You need to go upstairs and lie down.' I rattle my section of the newspaper to rouse him. 'Tell me, what's the story with Sam really? Why is she so crabbed all the time?'

'Sam? I don't know. She's unlucky in love, I think.' He yawns.

'She's bloody well unpleasant, is what she is; I never feel comfortable around her. Is she with someone?'

'A married chap from the hippy commune. He's a nice lad.'

'They are a harlequin pair, then, if he's nice. She's a right yoke.'

'Sam's all right,' Struan mutters, eyes closed again, his head drifting to my shoulder.

My low mood seeps forward into the night; it is early when we climb the stairs to Struan's bedroom in the eaves and, once in the bed, we turn away from each other. I wake in the night and snuff my nose into the pillow; I smell my own hair mousse and the residue of old skin. For a moment I am back in my Dublin bedsit and Dónal's bulk is radiating at me from the other side of the bed; my gut heats with pleasure at the thought of him. I toss my arm out and feel Struan's cool shoulder. The moon throws fat cuts of light into the room. I turn and look at the salmon-silver strands on the back of Struan's head; he is neatly tonsured, red scalped. I shiver and draw back my hand.

Chapter Six

I was belligerent the day of Dónal's funeral; anger choked me like a neck brace. I wasn't angry with Dónal for going and dying on me, but with the grief stealers who had lurched out of their caves to come and gawp. We knew loads of them growing up, but they never bothered with Dónal and he would not have wanted them there. A girl he had shifted once – Audrey – sat at the end of the first pew, sobbing like a madwoman. I was putting snowdrops for Dónal by the altar when I spotted her.

'I'm going to box that Audrey,' I said to Robin. 'What's she sitting there for?' He went over and asked her to move, telling her that pew was for family only. She shuffled out of it, and when she came near me I saw that she was wearing swathes of blue eyeliner and raspberry lipstick. I hated her for that. 'What fucker puts on a face for a funeral? Who is that poxy-well shallow?'

'Shush, Lillis,' Robin said, and shoved me down the aisle towards the door.

A lot of the mourners were home for Christmas and, since January had come, they were getting ready to go back to America or England or wherever they had returned from. Still, I couldn't believe the people who turned up; it was like the whole parish had hurried out to feed on gossip. Had Dónal Spain driven his motorbike into a wall on purpose? Where was he off to so late on New Year's Eve? Was he *on* something? Did the bike skid on ice or was he driving that bit too fast, the way fellas like him always do?

The older people irritated me as much as the younger ones. Outside the church, while we waited for the hearse, our neighbour

Mrs Cantwell stood beside Robin and me, rubbing her mittened hands together and blowing her breath out like a horse. She had the ease of the serial funeral-goer.

'He's in a better place now,' she said, 'he's with Our Lord.'

'Dónal didn't believe in God,' I said.

'I heard he was in a bog of depression, God love him. He's happier now.'

'How could he be happy?' I said. 'He's fucking-well dead.'

Robin grimaced at Mrs Cantwell, took me by the arm and brought me back into the church. 'Don't mind that old gee bag,' he said.

'They're annoying the shite out of me, Rob. All of them.'

'I know, I know. The things people come out with. Macker said to me last night, "I always knew Dónal Spain would die young." How I didn't reef the head off him.'

'Macker's an arsehole. Why couldn't he have died instead?'

'Ah, come on, Lillis. Shush.'

'I mean it! It's so fucking stupid that Dónal is dead, so pointless.'

I looked around. We were standing under the station of Jesus nailed to the cross; his skin was waxy, his mouth silent, the same as Dónal at his wake the night before. He had looked like an effigy – a weird, still version of himself. His coffin stood in his mother's front room like an outsized ornament; Mr Spain was perched beside it, worrying the satin by Dónal's head with his fingers. I stood on the other side of the coffin saying, 'I don't believe this', over and over again. Dónal's older brother, Cormac, had made it home from Australia that morning. He slunk in the corner, watching me; his arms, sticking out from rolled-up shirtsleeves, were covered in tattoos.

Verity brought me home early because I couldn't stop crying. I stayed by the coffin for ages, sobbing, with my hand on the suit that covered Dónal's broken body; Verity said I was upsetting the Spains. Cormac hugged me hard before we left; he stank of new sweat on top of stale, but he had his brother's shape, so I let him hold me and weep into my hair. I liked the feel of him wrapped around me; I could pretend he was Dónal.

Dónal came to my bedsit the week before he died to look at some pictures I had done. I was putting together a project on men's faces for my photography course. I had shot Dónal and Mr Spain together; Robin and Anthony sat for me too.

Dónal perched on my bed and flicked through the photographs. 'There are no pictures of you,' he said.

'It's called "Men", my project. I told you that.'

'My face looks real wide in all of these.'

I snatched the album back. 'Don't be a sap. Why can't you say something nice? I think they came out great.'

'It's not your fault that I've got a humongous head. Quasimodo,' he said, and lurched across the room. He mooched around, poking at the snow globes I had lined up on the mantelpiece. 'Lillis, when are you going to go with me? Properly, I mean.'

'Ah, Dó, we've been through this. We'd drive each other mental.'

He came and knelt in front of me, took my face in his hands. 'You wouldn't drive me mental,' he said, and kissed me.

He pushed my legs apart and jiggled towards me. I could feel his cock hard against my pubic bone. I kissed him back. Part of me loved the familiarity of being with him, but he was Dónal Spain. Good old Dónal. He was too close to me for the mess and upheaval and sparkle of love. He had peed in my tea set when I was six; set fire to my doll's house on purpose, and given me Chinese burns almost weekly since we were tots. We had swapped duffel coats so often as kids neither of us knew who owned which. And we were different: he was laddish and cheery; I was melancholic and bookwormy. We had little in common but our long history and the place we had grown up in.

The shadows from the bedside lamp made Dónal's face look puckish. He stood up and swung on top of me and pressed his hands to each side of my head. He bounced up and down, making the bedsprings grunt. I laughed and struggled against his grip; the mattress valleyed under our weight and Dónal moved again, pushing his body down on me. His thighs felt strong along my sides and I thought how beautiful he looked, so rounded out and well made, like a grown-up cherub. I pushed my hands against his and swung him over, so that I was on top. He thrust against me.

'No, no. Be still,' I said. I pulled off my T-shirt, unclipped my bra and swung my breasts over his face; he lunged upwards, but I pulled back before his mouth could reach them. I did this again and again until he clamped his lips around one nipple. I laughed, let him suckle for a moment, then unhooked his mouth with one finger. I looked into his face. 'I want to tell you something.'

'Hmm?'

'I've been offered a job in a hotel in Scotland for next summer,' I said, straightening my spine and pincing him with my knees.

'Oh?'

'Yeah.'

I wriggled and he let go of my hands and I lifted off him; I lay down and put my head on his chest.

'Are you going to go?' he asked.

'It's something different. An opportunity. I don't know.'

'What's not to know? A summer in Scotland.'

'I suppose.'

Dónal combed his fingers through my hair, down my neck. 'It's a mistake, really, isn't it, to fall in love with your fuck-buddy?'

I squinted at him. 'Is that what we are? Fuck-buddies? I thought we were friends.' I opened his shirt, pushed up his vest and ran my finger down the line of hair that tangled from his belly button to his crotch, then looked into his face. 'Do you love me, Dónal?'

'I think so. Yeah.' He kissed my nose. 'I'd marry you, you know.'

'Oh stop,' I said, sitting up and pulling on my T-shirt. 'You're too young to be talking about marriage.'

'And are you?'

'I have years ahead of me for all that.'

He hugged me, burying his nose in my hair. 'I *do* love you, you know.' Dónal smiled, took me by the waist and pulled me back onto him. 'Marry me, darling,' he said, in his film-star voice.

'Shut up.'

Dónal turned my body over; he pulled my T-shirt over my head again and mounded his palm over my bum, along my spine, up over my shoulder blades. He fingered the tattoo of a quaver that nestled on my neck just below the hairline; a crooked image with blurry lines, like all badly drawn tattoos. It was a folly I had hidden from my parents but which, for me, sang to my love for music. Dónal kissed the tattoo.

'It's like a little sperm,' he said.

'What?'

'Your quaver; it looks like a swimmer. A spermatozoon.'

'Trust you to come up with that.' I shrugged him off, crawled to the end of the bed and sat there.

'Come on,' Dónal said.

He stripped to his vest and boxers and we got under the covers. He nosed at my neck saying, 'Nuzzle, nuzzle, nuzzle' – a silly saying we shared – and I laughed and pulled his vest over his head, tossing it onto the floor. I loved to feel his chest flush with mine; it was familiar, heavy, comforting. We kissed for ages, then moved together, contemplatively and carefully, taking our time. Afterwards I could smell the bitter salt of our sex from his body. His face was lopsided on the pillow and his cheeks pink in a way that they only ever were when we lay in bed together after sex. He pushed one hand through my hair.

'Think about what I said, Lillis. I want you to be my girlfriend, officially like.' He kissed my lips. 'I don't know what I'll do if you say no. I might go away myself.'

The day after the funeral, I wore Dónal's vest to bed, trying to slip him on like a second skin. In the middle of the night I woke, worried that my smell would cancel out his smell, so I took off the vest, rolled it up and used it as a pillow. I couldn't cry; I hadn't cried since the wake. Robin wept throughout the funeral Mass and I held onto his waist, feeling responsible for him but also irritated by him. He and Dónal had drifted over the years – what was making him cry so much? What right had he to act like he was the one suffering?

I was demolished by Dónal's death; I couldn't understand it. How could he be gone? It did not make sense. People like Dónal didn't die.

I drifted back to sleep where I dreamt he was with me in my bedsit; I couldn't reach him and he wouldn't speak when I spoke to him. But he was alive and with me. Still, I felt uneasy in the dream, knowing there was some untruth in it; that something impossible was taking place. I woke suddenly, sat up in bed and laughed aloud at the idiotic notion that Dónal was no more. No. It couldn't possibly be. But my face was tight from the strain of the previous few days and Dónal's vest was on my pillow and I knew it was true.

Chapter Seven

I stride ahead of Struan, up the track. Globs of heather tuft from the verges and the hills above us lie like resting rabbits.

'Will we stop for a wee minute?' he calls.

'Are you wrecked?' I say, turning to look at him. He sits on a rock and pulls on a cigarette. 'Look at you puffing on that thing like a dirty dragon. It's no wonder you can't keep up.'

'I can keep up; I want to maintain a certain pace, that's all.'

'What's that – old man pace?' I walk down and stand over him.

'Less of that now, girlie.' He swipes at me with his hands and drags me onto his knees so that I straddle him. I can feel the prick of his leg hairs along the backs of my thighs. I look over his shoulder, down to the sea loch, which glisters like mica under the sun.

'How far have we walked, do you think?' I ask, rubbing Struan's shoulders; they are turning paprika from sunburn.

'Well, if you consider that a Kinlochbrack mile is actually two and a half miles, I'd say we've done about five.' He pushes me off his knees and gets to his feet.

'So two normal miles. It feels like more. Is it too early to have our lunch?'

Struan sucks the last blast from his cigarette, stubs it out and puts the butt under a rock.

'Yes, Miss Yourell, it's far too early for lunch.' He grabs me around the waist and kisses me deeply. 'You look sexy in that vest. Maybe we should find a soft spot among the heather.'

'We're supposed to be doing something different today.'

'Outdoor sex *is* different.'

'I don't want spiders and things crawling on me; I wouldn't be able to concentrate.'

'OK, OK. We'll go on.'

We walk hand in hand further up the path. The higher we go, the more of Kinlochbrack we can see, spread like a toy town below us, its streets a perfect grid. Struan tries to point out his house to me, but all I can see is a blur of rooftops. He counts the streets back for me to get to Clanranald Street and I pretend to see his house to keep him happy. We see Tom's white van drive away from the Strathcorry.

'There's Tom, delighted now after giving Dulcie the old one-two in the walk-in fridge,' Struan says.

'What? I didn't know Dulcie and Tom were together.'

'More like untogether.'

'Funny, I thought Tom was married.'

'He is. But you might as well try to tie sand with a rope as understand the love life of the average Kinlochbracker.'

'Well, that's for sure.'

We walk on and the muscles in my calves pull and ache. I can feel the sun parching my face and I stop to rub on sunscreen; Struan refuses to use any and I am telling him how foolish he is when an obese rat runs past us along the verge, quickly followed by a stoat. I jump sideways and squeal. The rat lollops like a squat pony and disappears into the heather, the stoat chasing close behind.

'See what could have run over us if we were having sex on the ground? Ugh!'

'They have more on their minds than a couple of humping humans. That rat is dinner.'

'Now you're turning me off my lunch.'

The pine-soaked air is thin and cool in my nostrils as I trot ahead of Struan into a stand of trees. My skin feels like a shrinking balloon when the cold of the forest instantly dries the sweat on my body. Struan jogs up behind me and closes his arms around my waist.

'I've got you now,' he says, close into my ear.

I shrug off my backpack and let it fall to the ground; I turn to him and we kiss fiercely. Struan pushes me towards a tree and spins me around to face it; he places my two hands on the trunk. The bark is gnarly under my palms and the damp smell of old wood envelops my face. Struan's fingers fumble with the button on my shorts, so I undo it for him and let them slip to my ankles. I can feel heat radiating from his body to mine and his breath spurts on my ear in short, sharp blasts. He kneads my breasts with both hands and slips his cock inside my knickers, making me gasp; I push back against him and he groans. Our sex is furious, quick, my knees buckle forward and I press my hands into the tree to stay standing. When Struan comes, we break away from each other panting.

'Whoo!' he says. 'If the hike didn't kill me, that would have. Mother of Divine.'

I laugh and go to kiss him, but he is already bent over his bag and taking out the picnic blanket. He tosses it on the ground and lies down.

'*Now* can we have our lunch?' I say, pulling up my shorts and re-hooking my bra.

'Oh, go on then,' he says, and lights a cigarette. He has one arm across his eyes and is working hard to steady his breathing.

When he has smoked his fag, we sit and eat the egg rolls I have made and drink bottles of beer. I hand Struan a slice of Ecclefechan tart and I eat another; the fruit in it is juicy and the pastry heaves with butter.

'Everything tastes so fine,' Struan says, 'after sex in the forest.' He laughs, rustles in his bag and produces a Kendal Mint Cake. 'You can't go for a Highland walk without mint cake,' he says, tearing the plastic wrapper and handing me a jagged white lump. 'Even walkers on Everest have to have their Kendal's.'

'That sounds like a jingle.'

I let the sugary cake melt on my tongue then I breathe quickly through my nose to feel the sharp mint in my nostrils. We lie in each other's arms on the blanket when we are finished eating and Struan snoozes while I listen to the sounds of the wood, the small rustlings and snappings. I hear the call and echo of a bird that I don't recognise. The cold, clay smell all around reminds me of exploring woods with Dónal, until we were both scared rigid by stray sounds and the dark between the trees. Anthony had told me there were bears in the woods and though I knew it couldn't be true, there was always that doubt. What if? Those thoughts caused a sudden need to pee, but I would hold it until we got away from the wood to the safety of the fields and sunlight. Once clear of the trees, Dónal would act like nothing frightened him, but his laugh was sour and nervy and I knew he was as jumpy as I was.

I kiss Struan's mouth to rouse him but he keeps his eyes shut, so I poke him awake with my fingers.

'Stop jabbing me, Lillis.'

'I want to walk on.'

He groans but pulls himself up; we pack our things before moving through the trees. I slide my arm around his waist, loving the protective heft of him. The ground is springy like a good carpet and I bounce my feet to make the most of the feeling. I have that perfect after-food, after-sex heaviness: my limbs are dull and my stomach is packed, but I feel warm and free too. I gently bite Struan's arm and he ruffles my hair.

In a clearing, we come across a group of pheasant huddled together like delegates at a conference. I stop, put my hands out and sing to them, a few lines of a country song that has been swinging in my head for days, about singing an old-fashioned song.

The pheasant patter about, knocking into each other, then huffle away like tiny grannies, looking put out.

'We should grab a few and take them to Dulcie – get her to cook them up,' Struan says.

'I would love to see you catching a pheasant. Off you go.' I push him. 'Go on.'

'I'm not in the mood,' he says, laughing.

Tom has told me there is a heavy fog forecast; I want to catch it on film, so I get up at six in the morning. It is cold and my head feels swimmy. I fumble through my bag of clean clothes and find a thick, plaid shirt of Struan's, put there in error by the girls at the inn's laundry. It makes me smile to find it among my things and I put it on over a T-shirt and jeans; I take my camera and leave the staff house.

The fog sits like a quilt over the village; Loch Brack is obscured and so are the hills. It is as if Kinlochbrack has been sliced off the world and set adrift under a cloud. I like the feeling of that very much; it adds to the Sunday calm. The streets are silent and my footsteps bang and echo, echo and bang; it is nice hearing my own noise thrown back to me. In the distance, I can hear the tok-tok of the boats in the harbour; the fishermen are, as usual, the only other people about.

I walk up a silent Clanranald Street; the houses emerge from the fog one by one as I make my way along the terrace. I cross the road to take a picture of the brass ship's wheel outside the chandler's; its spokes drip mist like tears. A door slams and I recognise the bash of the brass knocker and the scrape-squeal of Struan's front door. I turn to see if he will come along the path opposite me, heading for the inn; I lean forward, smiling, getting ready to call out to him. I form the shape of his name on my tongue. Sam emerges from the fog, her head bent low under the hood of her jacket. I slip back against the wall of the chandler's and watch her disappear into the fog further along Clanranald Street.

A visiting play in the town hall has attracted a pre-theatre crowd to the bistro. We have never been as busy and while sweat slides down my face and back, midges eat me under my bra and inside my knickers. I keep having to leave the bistro and run into the kitchen to scratch. It is one of those hellish nights where the diners are high-spirited and demanding, the stereo is too loud, jigging out its Scottish tunes, Sam acts bossy and Dulcie is in a rage.

'Lillis, table five are waiting an age for that wine,' Sam says, shoving past me to scrape and stack plates for the kitchen porter, by the back sink. 'The Pouilly-Fumé?'

'I know what wine they ordered, Sam, and I'm getting it.' I rub fiercely at midge bites through my tights.

'Don't bother,' she says, going to the wine locker.

'I said I'd get it. Can you just leave off?' I grab the bottle from her hand.

'Relax,' she snaps, and stalks off.

'Service!' Dulcie shouts, and I know that if I don't pick up the plates immediately she will roar at me. I leave the unopened wine bottle down as Struan swings past, with a tray of bread baskets.

'All right, hen?' he says.

I turn my back to him and go deeper into the kitchen to collect the order from Dulcie.

'Table eight,' she says. 'Come on, come on, come on. Don't stand there like a clump of muck.'

I take up the plates and serve table eight, a well-dressed foursome. One of the women lifts their wine bottle to refill the glasses.

'Oh, look at this. The label says "Prosecco is the imprisoned laughter of charming maidens". That's hilarious, isn't it?'

All four laugh and then they look at me, wanting me to join in. I force a smile but am reminded of table five's wine, abandoned in the kitchen. I rush away and charge through the swing doors. Sam and Struan are there and she is dangling the Pouilly-Fumé in front of him.

'I said I'd bring it to them and Lillis more or less told me to fuck off,' she says.

'That's not what I said at all.' I reach for the bottle and she pulls it away.

'Ah-ah. I'll handle this,' Sam says.

I look at Struan and he raises both palms.

'Jesus. Thanks, Struan. Just fucking thanks,' I say, and, realising I am about to cry, I dash through the kitchen, out to the staff hut.

Two of the other staff are in there, smoking. I don't want to have to talk to anyone so I sit on the step outside, wiping at my tears and snot with my shirtsleeve. Midges hang around the yard-light like a swaying puff of dandelion snow; I get up and swing my hand through the cloud to scatter them.

'Little midgie bastards,' I shout.

I hear Struan laugh behind me. 'That's a rubbish effort. You seem to be having a bad night all round.'

'What the fuck was that with Sam?'

'Sam gets het up; she wants it all to run smoothly.'

57

'We all want that; I was doing my best. You might have stood up for me.'

'Let it go, Lillis; it's no big deal.' He lights a fag, snorts and spits. 'Ahhh. There's nothing like a busy bistro to make me a happy, happy man.'

'I saw her, you know, coming out of your house on Sunday morning. I saw Sam.'

Struan holds his cigarette in mid-air, then takes a drag. 'And?'

'What do you mean "and"? What the fuck is going on, Struan?'

'There's nothing going on, Lillis, and I'm getting kind of pissed off telling you that.'

'Well, what am I supposed to think? It was half six in the morning.'

'Sam meets her boyfriend at my house when he comes across from the commune at Scoraig. End of.'

'Why does she meet him at your house?'

'Because he's married. Because they have privacy at mine that they can't get at the staff house. Because there's a double bed in my spare room. Because she's a mate.'

'She's a sly cow.'

'In your opinion,' Struan says, and flicks his cigarette into the sand bucket that is spilling butts. 'Back to work, eh? It's busy.' He grabs me in a hug and I endure it, though I want to thump him. He wipes at the tears that are slipping again from my eyes. 'Your bladder is near your eye, Yourell.'

'You sound like my father.'

Struan pinches my cheeks and stares into my eyes before kissing me hard.

'Back to work. And take it easy on Sam.'

I arrive back into the kitchen in time to hear Dulcie shout 'Service!' and I go and pick up the plates.

Margaret reminds me of a half-mad, half-benevolent nun who taught me in school – she has the same stack of near-perfect teeth that Sister Albert used to grind robustly whenever she was annoyed with someone in class. Margaret frisses the fingers of one hand through her hair and spoons globs of baby rice into Charlie's mouth with the other.

'I just don't believe that Sam is Struan's type,' she says.

'They used to go out.'

'Briefly. As in for a couple of weeks, if memory serves.'

'I can't stand her. She's sneaky, you know? All sweetness and light in front of Struan, but bitching at me behind his back. And she's a queer hawk – shifty. I wouldn't trust her if my life depended on it.'

Charlie waves his arms – they are so pudgy it looks like there are elastic bands pinching his wrists and elbows. Margaret scrapes the spoon up Charlie's chin, dragging at the mulchy rice he has burbled out through his lips.

'Och, you're a mess, wee man,' she says, then turns to me. 'She would mind mice at a crossroads, that Sam.'

I giggle. 'I haven't a clue what that means, but it sounds about right.'

'I mean she's cunning and capable. A bitch.'

'Language, Margaret!' We both laugh, which makes Charlie chuckle too.

'Are you laughing, wee boy? What's so funny?' She sweeps Charlie out of his bouncer and whips off his bib in one expert movement. 'Let's take him out for a walk.'

Margaret's devotion to her baby son amazes me. My memories of childhood are of benign neglect – I am sure Verity never ever took such interest or care with Robin or me. She certainly didn't talk to us when we were little, the way Margaret and Gordon talk to Charlie, as if he deserves inclusion in all that happens in their world. He is not yet a year old, but he is as important to them as any adult. Our home was one of silences and bad humour; Verity so clearly resented being a mother that she took it out on Robin and me.

'Mummy and Lillis are taking Charlie for a walk,' Margaret says, buttoning him into his jacket and pinching gobbets of snot from his nose with her fingers. These she flicks into the air. 'Maybe Charlie will see a seal. A seal! Will Charlie see a seal in the harbour?' She snugs her forehead against his and he chortles, showing his tiny teeth, all four of them. His mouth is still crusted with rice and he drools onto his chin, and I wonder how Margaret puts up with all his leaky, stinky, endless dirt.

Margaret lets me push the buggy down Market Street and along Shore Street; she swings her arms and proclaims herself useless. She tells me about her mother, about her cancer and her death, about how close they were. I get bored pushing the buggy after a while and Margaret takes over. She relaxes as soon as her fingers close over the handles; she seems restored. I tell her about Dónal; that I'm not sure what way to grieve for him.

'I don't know whether I'm going to feel this bad forever, or if at some point it will be easy to think about him,' I say. 'Think about him lightly, you know, without feeling pain? Grief is so hard.'

'It sure is; grief is work, it's an active thing. Where do we put it all? The memories, the sadness, the constant feeling of loss. The dead only continue to exist because we talk about them, right?'

'You don't believe in an afterlife?'

'I believe in the rebirth of souls, Lillis. Something of my mother lives on in Charlie, I'm sure of it.'

I look at Charlie, at his moony face, and find it hard to believe that somewhere inside his fat little body, so soft and open to the world, lies the residue of his Irish granny.

'Dónal didn't believe in any of that, so I don't really either.'

'But you feel Dónal around you, don't you?'

'I suppose. Well, yes, in my dreams. At night especially, that's when I sense him close by.'

'So, you see, he hasn't left you. Not completely.' We do a circle of the village and by the time we are back to Market Street, Charlie is fast asleep in his buggy. Margaret lets us into her house and, after parking Charlie in the hall, we sit in the soft light of her kitchen, listening to the kettle boil. 'I suppose you have to ask yourself where Struan fits into all of this. Is he replacing Dónal?'

I look at Margaret, at her amiable, searching face and I realise that I do not have an answer to her question. I shrug and she gets up to brew the tea.

Chapter Eight

Verity sent my father to tell me that Dónal was dead. Dónal had asked me to go to a New Year's Eve party with him, in some flat off the South Circular Road. He gave me the address and I said I would see him there, but I had gone to the pub with my college friends and didn't make it. When my buzzer rang on New Year's Day I thought it was Dónal, come to give out and tell me what a great night I had missed.

I leapt from my bed, pressed the intercom button and hopped back under the covers. After a minute or two, the door opened and Anthony stood there, not speaking.

'Dad?' I pulled my dressing gown from the end of the bed and wrapped myself into it. I was footless the night before and aches were clawing at the inside of my face, my mouth and my brain. I pointed at my head. 'Hangover. But Happy New Year.'

Anthony nodded and stepped into my bedsit, closing the door after him. 'Lillis, I have news; it's not good.'

I jumped towards him. 'What? Is it Verity? Robin?'

'No, they're fine. Look, Lil, there's been an accident.' He put me sitting on the bed and then sat beside me, his arm around my shoulder.

'You're freaking me out. Is it the boys?' I was sure something had happened to one of the two sons he had with India.

'No, not the boys. Lillis, Dónal Spain came off his motorbike last night and I'm afraid it was fatal. He died instantly.'

'What? No.' I looked at Anthony to see why he was saying this to me. 'That's ridiculous. No.'

'I'm sorry, Lillis. It happened along the canal in the early hours of this morning. His bike hit a wall.'

I could hear what my father was saying but holding onto the truth of it, the facts of what he had said, was like trying to grip a wet eel. I shook my head.

'No, no, no.' I wanted to climb back into bed and I wanted Anthony to go away. I laughed. 'I'm dreaming,' I said, relieved, and I grabbed at my father, sure he would not be there at all. My hand clutched the hairy back of his hand and he took hold of my fingers, pumping them up and down as if I were a child again and we were playing a game.

'He's gone, Lillis. I'm sorry. Look, why don't you get dressed and come to Verity's with me? You can go and see the Spains. They'll need all the support they can get. You should be there; they'll want you there.'

The fish and salt smell of the Atlantic wound its way up the narrow streets that were still cold and early-morning empty. Pedestrians dodged the delivery trucks that hulked everywhere, while shopkeepers sluiced the dirt and vomit from their entryways with buckets of water that stank of Jeyes Fluid. The train had left me at the bottom of Eyre Square and I strolled down to Quay Street to meet Anthony for breakfast. Verity had suggested I go to Galway to visit my father after I had spent night after night at her house, lolling in bed, missing Dónal and feeling sorry for myself.

It was India who greeted me, from her flumped position inside the doorway of the Café du Journal; she stood when she saw me and stretched out her hand.

'Anthony had to meet with one of his students – some minor emergency. You'll have to make do with me for now.' India gave a small smile; her teeth were luminous inside the lilac slick of her lips.

'That's OK,' I said, gripping India's hand and kissing her ripe cheek, 'it's lovely to see you.' India smelt sweet and musky, like cedar or something else old and precious. 'How are you? And the kids?'

India shook her wrists, making her silver bangles rattle. 'I am fine, they are fine. Tim is in big school now, he's very proud of himself.'

'Aw, sweet, I bet he looks cute in his uniform. Tiny Tim. How's my father?'

'Oh, you know Anthony, working too hard as always, but he is well. His department may have made an important discovery, something to do with seaweed. I'll let him tell you himself.' India drained her coffee. 'How is your mother?'

'Oh, she's annoying everyone around her, as usual. Herself most of all.'

'Poor Verity.'

I ordered toast and two cappuccinos. The air was silent between us while we stirred our coffee; I let tan nuggets of sugar melt on my teaspoon before dunking it low and stirring it through.

'Did you know that cappuccinos are called after the Capuchin friars, because the coffee is the same colour as their habits?' I said.

India laughed. 'That's the sort of thing Anthony would say; he is full of titbits of trivia. No, I didn't know that, but I will remember it from now on.' She placed her hand on my knee. 'I was sorry to hear that your friend passed away. He was so young. How have you been?'

I looked away. 'OK. Sort of.'

'It is devastating for his family. To lose a son. My goodness.' She wrung her hands.

We talked about work: India's with underprivileged children and her dealings with social workers; my bored frustration with the camera shop. The café warmed up; customers belched in and out through the door, delivering wafts of bleachy air and the screeking of gulls as they did. Anthony bustled through eventually, mouthing a sorry and holding out his palms in mock attrition; he leaned over the table.

'My two best girls, all cosy.' He stooped forward, kissed India on the mouth, then me on the top of my head. 'How are you, darling?'

'I'm all right,' I said, frowning then smiling. I was determined not to be low while I was in their house; my father could never cope with bad humour.

'You look tired. Come on, let's get you home.'

Anthony carried my backpack and linked us both for the short stroll to the Long Walk. Their house overlooks the Claddagh Basin where the River Corrib empties itself with force into the sea. Once indoors, I curled into the window seat in the sitting room to watch the huge cast of swans that bounced on the water, like players in a wet and windy theatre. I thought of the legend of the Children of Lir – the four swan children – Fionnuala and her three brothers, tossing on cold seas for hundreds of years. The girl acted as surrogate mother to her brothers, protecting them from all kinds of evil. I'm like Fionnuala, I thought, with my three brothers. Though I couldn't say that I knew Tim and Alex at all; they were so young, so far away. In truth, I barely registered them as family.

'I might take the boys out while I'm here. To Salthill, maybe.'

'Oh yes, they would like that very much,' India said, looking pleased. 'They are so fond of you and Robin, so proud. They tell everyone about their big sister and brother up in Dublin.'

'Do they really?' I felt a gush of heat in my stomach and smiled. Anthony winked at me.

'Do you think it's possible to ever get over losing someone? Like, *really* get over it?'

'Possible, but difficult,' Anthony said, and closed his eyes.

He looks like a psychiatrist sitting there, I thought, plump and wise. Even his fireside chair had the clichéd look of the TV shrink: its high, curved back sported thickly upholstered ears that seemed to hug the sides of his head. I took a deep breath, held it, then parped it out through my lips. My father opened his eyes and raised his eyebrows, inviting me to go on.

'I loved Dónal, you know, but I didn't love him the way he loved me. We were like brother and sister. Or on-off flat mates.' I dropped my chin to my chest. 'I was fond of him, *so* fond of him, but he drove me nuts. I miss him like crazy.'

'He was a good kid.'

I looked into the fire, at the petrol blue and white flames that were trying to find a hold on the stack of turf.

'It's as if he loved me too much; he loved all the love out of the two of us and I couldn't get a foothold, you know?' Anthony looked at me. 'All I know is that at some point, I gave up trying to take him seriously as a potential boyfriend. But now I can't understand that. I don't know why I didn't make the effort to love him, to be with him the way he wanted.'

'We don't choose who to love,' Anthony said.

I lifted my eyes to his and nodded. Anthony leaned over, took my hand and pulped my fingers through his own, hurting me – he was never aware of his own strength.

'Maybe I'll find someone to love, I don't know. I look at you and India and the boys, at how happy and content you are, and I think, "Anything is possible." '

'It took a long time to land where we are now, Lil, a long time. Don't forget that Verity and I went through hell. And India and I behaved badly through it all, by getting together in the first place.' He squeezed my hands. 'Life is long. Don't be in too much of a rush.'

'I'm not in a rush, I'm just saying.'

I could feel the scald of tears plucking at the backs of my eyes. I didn't want to cry in front of Anthony; he never knew what to say or do when people cried. It made him impatient.

'Look, a little holiday here, away from Dublin and memories, and away from Verity, might help. We'll only talk about Dónal if you want to. But we're here for you, darling, India and me.'

'Thanks, Dad.'

'What are you to us?' Alex asked, shoving his fists into his pockets when I held out my hand to him. The wind swished around my ears, throwing my hair into my eyes, and I clawed it away, peeling back the strands that had stuck to my lipstick. Tim held onto me tightly, as if afraid he would be thrown off the promenade into the churning sea.

'I'm your sister, Alex. You know that.'

'You're very old to be our sister,' he said, needling his black eyes at me. 'You could be someone's mum you're so old.'

'Could be, but amn't.' I forced a smile. 'I'm your half sister, but that makes it sound as if I'm half a person and I don't really like that.'

'It sounds OK to me,' Alex said, and turned to look across the bay at the low hump of County Clare. I looked at his tufty hair and the polished coffee colour of his neck. I examined Tim, his identical miniature. They are beautiful kids, I thought.

'The sea is lovely, isn't it? Wild,' I said, smiling at the boys.

Alex pointed across the water to Black Head. 'Daddy drives us over to there in his car. Do you have a car?'

'No.'

Alex smirked then looked away. 'I want to go home now.'

'I don't want to go home yet,' Tim said. 'She's bringing us for chips now, aren't you, Lillis?'

I nodded. 'Come on, Alex, give me your hand.' The boy snorted and hopped onto the cluster of rocks that formed the breaker wall above the sea. He looked back at me and Tim, then jumped from rock to rock, his open jacket flipping like a wimple in the wind. 'Alex, you're going to fall.' He glanced around at me and made a face, then turned back to jump forward again. His foot got caught in a crevice and he fell hard. He crouched there, no sound coming from him. I sprang over and dragged him upright. 'You're OK, Alex, you're all right,' I said, and he whimpered in my arms, his body tense.

I lifted his palms to see the damage: there was a lattice of scrapes and the inky bulge of fresh bruises. When Tim saw his brother's hands, he started to cry and I pulled him into the crook of my other arm. The three of us sat in a huddle on the rocks, the sea whipping behind; the boys cried and I sheltered them from the wind, trying to form properly comforting words to say to them.

Tim slurped his milkshake. 'Mummy says you are exactly like your mother.'

I looked over at him. 'Oh, really? What else does she say?'

'She says you *like* being sad. She said that to Daddy last night.' Alex robbed a chip from Tim's plate and he started to screech. 'Give it back, Alex, give it back. Lillis, he took one of my chips!'

I looked out through the café window at the frothy waves that were throwing themselves up onto the prom. Power walking women in bright fleece tops leapt to dodge them and pounded on up the seafront to where Salthill fizzled out. The sea fell back for a moment before heaving over the rocks again.

'What's *your* mother to us, Lillis?' Alex said.

'What? Oh, nothing; she used to be married to your dad, that's all. She's not related to you in any way.'

'She might be our stepmum,' Tim said doubtfully, picking at his chips with his fingers.

'I think she's our auntie. Daddy calls her Auntie Verity sometimes.'

'I said she's nothing to you,' I snapped, 'she's not a relative. And be glad of it.' I pointed at Tim. 'Use your fork.' The two boys stared at me and I stared back, swallowing hard. 'Let's go,' I said, standing up. Tim looked at his half-full plate but said nothing. We trooped out of the café and I walked ahead of them to the bus stop.

'I'm getting the train at six.' I stood in the doorway of Anthony's den.

'Come in, Lil, you look a bit off. What's happened?'

'I'm not *off*.' I pinched the door between my fingers and swung it backwards and forwards. 'And why do you always have to comment on how you think I'm feeling, anyway? I really fucking hate that – it's enough to put me in a bad mood. Every time I talk to you, I feel like I have to compose my face in a way that won't have you reaching for a psychology book.'

'Sorry, but clearly there *is* something wrong.'

'Jesus, I said I was all right.' I caught the handle and slammed the door; I marched to my room and started to pack. Anthony came to my bedroom and knocked on the door; when I didn't answer, he let himself in.

'The boys said they had a really nice time with you today. They enjoyed themselves hugely.'

'Really?'

'Yes. They loved the slot machines. We don't normally let them go into Caesar's Palace; India's quite strongly anti-gambling.'

'You could hardly call adding a few coins to a waterfall of five pence pieces "gambling". Good God.' I threw books and my camera into my backpack. 'India seems to be anti a lot of things. Including me.'

'What? She's not anti you; she's very fond of you.'

'That's not what Tim and Alex say. If they're to be believed, it seems India thinks I'm a morbid wreck. As is Verity.'

Anthony sighed. 'I think you might be exaggerating a bit. She's worried about you, that's all.'

'Well, tell her to stuff her worrying up her hole.'

'Ah, Lillis.'

'And also to stop bitching about my mother. She has no right.' I sat on the bed and started to cry. 'Oh fuck. What am I going to do, Dad? I think I'm going crazy.' Anthony sat beside me and pulled me to him. 'I let Dónal down and he might have killed himself over it. I feel so rotten about it all the time, so guilty. It's bad enough missing him without thinking it's all my fault as well.'

'Look, it seems like the end of the world at the moment, but it isn't. Things will get easier. Dónal's death was an accident.' He kissed my hair. 'You will survive this, I promise you will.' He hugged my side to his. 'And Lil, fuck the guilt – you only live once.'

I kissed Anthony on the cheek. 'Thanks, Dad. Verity's a basket case at the moment; she's acting like Dónal's death has affected her really deeply, but I know it's just an excuse to get gee-eyed. She won't tolerate *me* being sad either; it drives me mad.'

'Your mother is one of my favourite people on earth, Lillis, but, like all supremely selfish people, she's very, very hard to live with. I still have such huge love for her, but I know what she can be like.'

'And India? What sort of love do you have for her?'

'India is a wonderful woman, I love her to bits. But Verity was my big love. The love of my life.' Anthony sighed. 'And don't you dare tell India that I said that.'

'I wouldn't, Dad, you know that. Do you have regrets?'

'Regret, like guilt, is a wasted emotion. Don't bother with it, Lillis. I try not to.' He hugged me again. 'Come on, my angel girl, you're staying on here, as planned, because I refuse to let you go back to face Verity yet. You're supposed to be getting away from things.'

'Thanks, Dad. I love you, you know?'

'I know you do, Lil, and I love you too.'

We sat on the bed watching a bevy of swans move along the river through the rain, their shiny, paddling bodies bright against the dark water.

'Look at them, shaking their fat arses,' Anthony said, cocking his head at the swans. 'I always think they must be constipated from all the stodgy white bread they eat. You're supposed to throw them cabbage you know, not bread.' He stretched and yawned. 'They get these pink bits on their wings when they eat too much wheat – it means they're not well.'

'Dad, am I like Verity?'

Anthony leaned away and looked into my face. 'You've always had something of that melancholic air that she has. It's actually the first thing about your mother that I noticed and it's probably why I fell in love with her. The difference is you don't need alcohol to come alive, like Verity does. People have always done it for you: your school friends and Robin. I see how tuned in you and Rob are to each other still – he knows how to get you laughing, he brings you out of yourself, makes you glow.'

'And Dónal – do you think he ever did it for me?'

'No, darling, not Dónal, not in the way you need. But I sort of only see it now.'

He took my hand. A shiver juddered through me and I sat on to watch the families of bobbing swans turning for shore and home.

Chapter Nine

I know Struan doesn't want to have sex again, but I push a bit anyway, just to see; he leans in, looks into my eyes, and unpeels my hands from his skin. He yawns.

'I'd better get over to the inn,' he says.

Other times I would persist, kissing him deeply and tucking my body over his while pinning his arms to the sides of his head. It annoys him to give in, but he seems glad when he does. Sex is our connection – the one thing that binds us when I feel like I haven't a clue what is going on with him. If he won't be open with me, I think, at least we can have decent sex.

He jumps out of the bed and pulls on his trunks. I watch the movement of the skin over his bones: Struan is slim with a firm fleshiness that I love. Whether we are lying, sitting, or standing together, my hands always find their way to the taut pouches of his chest, with the curls of grey hair thrown there like a scatter of question marks. I love to knead and press the skin there and, when he is naked, I kiss his chest over and over, tugging gently on his nipples with my teeth.

Traffic noise rises from Clanranald Street to the window and grows louder; a tight breeze makes the net curtain come alive. The chlorine smell of morning winds into my nose and makes me want to sneeze. I plough the bed covers around my arms, snuggling deeper to cover my cold shoulders.

'Come here,' I say, and Struan sits. I climb out from under the quilt, push him onto his back and lie down on top of him, the length of my body heavy on his. I plunge my lips to his neck and kiss it.

'You're my *strupac*,' I say. 'Isn't that a great word? Margaret taught me that, it means "sup of tea" in Gàidhlig.' I snuggle against his skin. 'I love you, Strupac.'

'Mmm,' he says, and kisses my nose, flicking at it with one finger, then he heaves himself from under me and stands. 'I'm gone or I'll be behind. See you later.'

I stay on in bed, listening to Kinlochbrack rouse itself. I doze and wake, and think about Struan, about that remove he keeps; he has slotted something small but immoveable between us. If I press him, he reels away. But, tomorrow he is taking me south to visit his mother and that means something, surely.

A low moon, like a leaping fish, hangs in the sky above the city and drizzle fuzzes the edges of buildings, cars and street lights. Everything feels different in Glasgow, I think, even the rain. It is a proper city with its odd mix of old and new: roads on stilts, flats, factories, chimneys and spires. It has a grubby aura – not dissimilar to home – but Glasgow scares me a little because it is so vast; bigger by far than Dublin and more industrial in its make-up.

I tuck my arm into Struan's and put my head on his shoulder. We are in town clothes: a dress and pumps for me; a light suit for him. It feels good to be out of jeans and sandals, out of my waitressing uniform; it makes us both buoyant, being away from the inn and its concerns. We are more inclined to laugh, to be kind to each other. The niggles of work and Sam and busyness are left behind in Kinlochbrack.

Carnival lights bump and whirl above and around us; the thumping music grinds into my brain. I peck with my fingers at the candyfloss in my hand. Pulling a clump of the sticky pink mess, I push it between Struan's lips; he grunts and lets it melt on his tongue.

'This stuff is vile,' I say. 'Do you want to go on the bumpers?'

We are lingering in front of the booth that has 'Dodgems' bannered in green letters below a neon woman's bare breasts. My stomach is a bit iffy after the Crazy Jumper. And my head. I have had too much sugar; too much spinning like a dervish on the rides; far too much fear that the whole shebang was going to collapse and kill us all. I plop the candyfloss into a bin. We stop and stand in the middle of a straggle of teenagers and young families; we hold each other face to face.

'You have a halo,' Struan says, and wipes the soft rain that clings to my hair. He takes me in his arms and kisses my mouth, while people flow on all sides of us. 'So how do you like Glasgow so far, Miss Yourell?'

'I love it,' I say, 'and I love you.'

Struan's mother lives in his childhood home off the Byres Road, a brick two-up, two-down which is painted a shrill pink. The poky, skewed front garden is lush with weeds; we stand outside the gate, looking at the house.

'My father would spin in his urn if he could see the state of the place,' Struan says, and sighs. He rings the bell and his mother opens the door instantly; she must have been waiting behind it.

'There you are, pet. It's dreich out there.' She kisses Struan who has bent his face to hers. 'Hello, dearie,' she says to me, grabbing me to her chest and kissing both my cheeks.

'Mum, this is Lillis. Lillis, Pearl.'

'It's lovely to meet you, Mrs Torrance.'

'You can call me Pearl, hen.'

She is a dolly-bird gargoyle, hunched over and wearing too much makeup; her dress is the soft grey worn by nuns but she is dripping with gold chains and she wears long, hooped earrings. She has clearly hemmed the dress herself – crooked blue stitches make a track around the skirt end like an unmade road. She looks wrong in the dress, odd and sort of sweet. She ushers us through the tiny hallway into her lounge.

Pearl asks how the drive was; if we saw any crashes. She says she will never get into a car again. She puts us sitting on the sofa, folds her arms and keeps her eyes off me as she chats to Struan – she relays news of relatives, sick and out of work; bits of local gossip: Mrs McKenzie is dead; the postman took a stroke and can't speak anymore; Napier's stopped stocking the crispy morning rolls Pearl loves until she complained and now they have them again. I focus on her mouth: she is wearing a frosted pink lipstick that makes her teeth look green.

'We all thought Struan was a fairy, of course. For years,' she says, turning to me. 'Then he married that Sheena. Well. We all know how that went.'

'Mum, don't start,' Struan says, and looks at me.

'Oh, she was a besom, that Sheena,' Pearl says, climbing into her armchair. 'Money mad and ugly as a man.'

'You were married?' I say.

'Briefly.'

I pull my eyes away from Struan's and look around the room. It is filled with gew-gaws of every level of tackiness: porcelain frogs, Spanish dolls, shell covered ashtrays, and a Niagaric fountain feature that makes me want to pee. A TV hums in the corner, the sound turned down low.

'You'll have tea,' Pearl says.

'Great,' I say, eyeing a hip-height statue of Jesus that jostles with a china Alsatian beside the hearth. Christ's mournful eyes are tilted heavenward, begging deliverance, probably, from the kitsch-fest.

'Struan, go and make the tea,' she says.

'You have a lovely home, Pearl.'

'Och well. You're from Ireland, hen. You lot love your guns and bombs, eh? Shooting children and all that.'

'I don't approve of any of that. It's got nothing to do with me.'

'Nothing to do with you? I was sure Struan said you were Irish. Whatever you say, hen.'

She turns to the TV and I rub my palms together and wonder how long we will have to stay. I flick my eyes across her boast wall: her wedding photo is there – she looks impossibly hopeful and her husband looks smug; beside that there is a picture of Struan and his brother Lewis in Communion outfits; then their Confirmation pictures, both wearing the same fawn suit with a scarlet rosette on its wide lapel; next to that sits Lewis in a cap and gown. There are no pictures of their sister, who died as a girl. I try to remember her name but it won't come to me.

Struan teeters in with a tray, a rigor-mortis-like grin on his face; he serves us and we sip in silence. Pearl sits, eating a biscuit, staring at me. Her mouth seems to cause her trouble; the chewing looks like an ordeal. She snaps a piece of biscuit with her fingers and sucks it.

'How many bairns has your mother got, pet?'

'Two. There is myself and my brother.'

'A pigeon's clutch.'

'My father calls it "a gentleman's family".' I laugh.

'And is he a gentleman, your father? That's the question.' She turns away. 'I take it you two will marry? Every woman wants her big day, Struan. Even if she's modern in her outlook. You know, *young*. People look down their snot at you when you're not married. I want my day in the sun as mother of the groom, and I want it while I can still walk.' She gives her tea a clanking stir and reaches for my hand. 'Talk sense into him, hen. He can't go on like this, it's not right.' She looks around and whispers. 'People will think you're living in sin. Or worse.'

'We don't live together,' I say, looking at her hand on mine, at the sun-aged skin.

'No one gives a shit about that stuff anymore,' Struan says. 'Lots of couples live together without being married. People don't care.'

'I care,' Pearl says, slapping the coffee table with one palm. '*I* care.' She picks up a cigarette and waggles it at me. 'I hope to God there's no improper conduct in the bedroom.'

'Ah, Mum,' Struan says, 'for goodness sake.'

'What was it your father used to say about people who lived together but never married? "Why would a man buy a cow when he can get a pint of milk?" That's what he'd say.' She wheezes. 'See that now; you'd need to think about that. *Why would a man buy a cow when he can get a pint of milk?*'

'Charming,' says Struan.

'I live in the staff house, Pearl, belonging to the inn. And Struan has his house on Clanranald Street.'

'Well, anyway.' Pearl flicks her lighter to the cigarette and puffs; she looks at me. 'If you play along with some men, they turn on you. You try to do what you think they want, then bam, they get nasty. Struan's not like that; he's a gentleman. Unlike his father. You thank your lucky stars, pet.'

I feel tired with her and for her. 'I know how lucky I am,' I say.

'That's tip-top, hen. Tip-top!' Pearl drags hugely on her cigarette and smiles her green-toothed smile. 'Oh, and you needn't tell Struan about our little conversation, all right? Promise?'

'I promise.'

Struan looks at me over the top of his tea cup and tosses his eyes up to Heaven.

'You'll eat with me,' Pearl says.

'We will; we'd love to.' She goes to the kitchen and I let out a puff of stress through my lips. 'Jesus Christ. What was all that?'

'Mad as a brush. She's worse than the last time I saw her.' Struan scratches his head. 'Her mind just lets loose. Along with her tongue.'

'So, you have a secret wife,' I say. '*Sheena.*'

'It's no secret – it didn't come up.'

'You might have mentioned her.'

'It was thirty years ago, Lillis; not exactly to the forefront of my mind.'

'I suppose you have slip-of-the-mind kids too?'

'Nope, no kids.' He looks at his watch. 'Jesus, I wish we could go.'

'Well we can't. Where is she now?'

'Mum?'

'Sheena.'

'Here somewhere, I think, in Glasgow.' He pushes the heels of his hands into his eyes and rubs for a long time; he looks at me. 'What do you make of the house?'

I glance around and grimace. 'Loch Ness meets the Vatican.'

Struan laughs. 'Tartan and saints a-go-go.' He puts his arm around my shoulder.

Pearl comes back in and serves toast and beans by candlelight, with silverware and orange juice and real napkins.

'Is this it?' Struan asks, when she has us all set up with trays on our knees.

'This is great, Pearl; perfect,' I say, 'don't mind him.' But she sits, her limbs wobbling, in silence. We start to eat but Pearl gets up slowly and leaves the room, carrying her tray before her like a sacrifice. 'Struan, what the fuck did you say that for?'

He goes after her and is gone ages; I hear the low thrum of their conversation coming through the wall. I eat my food and watch the silent TV, trying to lip read. There are no bookshelves; no newspapers or magazines to idle through. Struan comes back; Pearl doesn't reappear.

'She's having a wee lie down,' he says, his mouth in a grim line. 'She said to say goodbye. I had to promise that we'll stop by before heading for Kinlochbrack tomorrow.'

'That's OK.'

The hotel corridor smells like vinegar, reminding me of Verity's homemade cleaning products. Our room is stuffy, the heavy curtains and zealous central heating make the air dry and hot. I wake, irritable from trying to breathe in my sleep, but I am too lazy to get out of bed to open the window. My mouth is stale and my head throbs. Struan rolls over on top of me and slides my knickers down on my hips. I kiss him, ask him to go slow, be gentle.

'No fucking, just loving, OK, Struan?'

'OK, babe.' He licks my neck, dipping his tongue into the hollow at the base of my throat. 'You're so beautiful.'

'All that business with your mother freaked me out; I feel sick.'

I turn my head away from him and stick my nose into the stiff cotton of the pillowcase; I am glad it smells of nothing. Struan moves down my body, caressing and sucking. I pluck at the bedclothes with my hands and stare at the window, willing it to open and offer me some air. Struan is parting my thighs with his fingers.

'Lil, are you all right? Do you want me to stop?'

'No, no, don't stop. I need you; I need to feel you inside me.' I take his face in my hands, pull his body up along mine and kiss his forehead. I push my pelvis forward and guide him in.

Struan told Pearl we would call at lunchtime; again, he rings the door bell. It is one o'clock and when Pearl opens the door, she is still in her nightdress, her hair in rollers.

'Mum?'

'There's something terrible going on in London,' she says; she turns away from us and goes into the lounge.

'The old pair spent their honeymoon in London,' Struan says, as we hang our jackets in the hall, 'no doubt there's a tiny catastrophe to do with some place they visited; a tea shop closed down or something.'

I follow him into the lounge and, on the TV screen, see the destroyed front of Harrods department store. There is a wave of black smoke and a lone Bobby standing on the glass-strewn street.

'What the fuck?' I say.

'That's old footage,' Struan says. 'It's from a few years ago.'

'Your lot are at it again. There's been another bomb,' Pearl says, staring at me.

'They're not my lot.'

'Anyone dead?' Struan asks.

'I'm waiting to find out,' Pearl says. She points her finger at me. 'You ought to be ashamed, hen.'

'That's enough, Mum.'

'I'm only saying.'

'Well don't.'

We sit side by side on the sofa, staring at peach and grey smoke pluming out of the London Stock Exchange.

'Who?' I ask.

'"Who?" she says. The IRA. You can be sure of it.'

Pearl flicks the remote control to see which station has the latest. On each channel the newsreader has the same small updates: there was a warning; the building had been evacuated; there were no casualties.

'Thank God for that,' I say.

'Why is the child of one black and one white parent always called black?' Pearl says. 'Surely they're as white as they are black?'

I glance from her to Struan.

'Mum, what are you on about?'

'Look at him,' she says, pointing at the newsreader, 'he's neither here nor there.'

'I think we should head north now,' I say. 'It's a long drive.'

We all stand up. Pearl holds her eyes over our heads, so she won't have to look at us. She sits down and picks fluff from the sleeve of her dressing gown.

'I'll never understand you young people.' She looks back at the TV screen. The footage has changed: they are showing archive photos of more London bombings. 'We're only bodies, anything can happen.' Pearl waves at the images on the television. 'So there we are. Things can always get worse,' she says, more to herself than to us.

We say goodbye and she doesn't stir; she is like someone who has shut herself down. Struan kisses her head, tells her to take care and we leave.

Chapter Ten

My brain is thundering with a hangover. I am meeting Robin at the National Gallery and I am late. Robin makes no comment when I skitter up to him in the café, apologising and shaking my head.

'Where's the jacket I bought you?' I ask. 'I hate that frog-spawny one.' I pull at his collar and sit down beside him.

'I wish you wouldn't call it spawny. It sounds lewd.'

'And *you* object to lewd?' I hug him with one arm. 'I ming of booze. I went straight to Verity's last night from the airport and Anthony was there on a flying visit from Galway. Next thing you know the three of us are full of drink and carousing away. The two of them all reminisces and laughter. The things they said! My poor ears. We drank four bottles of wine between us and Anthony ended up staying the night. I rang your flat to get you to come over.'

'I was out. Is Anthony gone back to Galway?'

'After some conference thing today. You know, I looked at him and Verity at the breakfast table this morning, bickering madly and poking at each other's soft spots, but still fond of each other. It made me wonder what it would have been like if they'd stayed together. If we would have turned out differently.'

'You can't change the past,' Robin says.

'I know that.' I turn away from him, irritated. 'God, my head is lifting. If I puked I'd be the better for it.' My hangover has made my body alert and jumpy, as if it has forgotten how to be still.

'Come on.' Robin stands up and holds out his hand. 'A quick turn around your favourite paintings will sort you out. An eyeful of *Cupid and Psyche in the Nuptial Bower* will take that puss off your face. Won't it?' I grunt and Robin kneads my shoulder. 'Come on, Lillis.'

I feel groggy and narky, but my hangover grumpiness doesn't faze Robin; it's real grumps he can't handle. Standing up, I hug him hard.

'I've missed you, Rob.'

'So, when is this famous man of yours arriving?' he says. 'Highlander.'

'He flies in tonight.'

'I hope he's ready for the Yourells.'

'Oh stop. I'm as nervous as all fuck.'

We wander through a hall of marble sculptures, each erect pubescent form thrusting either a smooth breast or a reposing penis into my sightline. Robin seems off with me; there is a pull in the silence between us and I am not sure what to say to make things softer or easier. I stop in front of a statue of a supine couple, wrapped limb on limb around each other. Their white bums are puckered with tiny holes, probably from being rain-beaten in the garden of some Italianate villa. I touch the woman's cold skin.

'She's got cellulite on her arse,' I say, expecting Robin to laugh. He gazes at the sculpture, his face set and solemn. 'What's wrong with you, Rob?'

'Are you serious about this bloke? This *Struuuuu-an.*' He bugs his eyes, to show me he thinks it is a stupid name.

'Serious-ish. Why?'

'If you end up living in Scotland it means I have to stay here and mind Verity. Forever.'

'It doesn't, you know. She's not our responsibility.' I rock on my feet and look around at the other statues in the room. 'Half of these are eunuchs.' I point to the memberless hordes who stand nearby and make chopping motions with an imaginary blade.

'You know, the first time I came to the gallery was with Granny and Grandad Yourell,' Robin says. 'You must've been a baby. I remember coming into this room and Grandad's eyes lit up when he saw all the naked girls. Granny ran us through here, tutting and gabbling like a mad old hen, but I saw her wink at Grandad once we were out the other side.' He smiles. 'I miss them. They were great, in their way.'

'You're very maudlin today, Rob. Cheer up, I'm only home for a few nights. You won't be stuck looking after Verity. I promise. I'll make sure.'

I decide it is safest if Struan meets Verity outside of her own home. She is unlikely to arrive drunk to a restaurant but I can't be sure she doesn't have a secret stash in her house that she would lay in to, for courage, if I bring Struan there. She is impressed with his choice of restaurant on Saint Stephen's Green and is gracious in accepting his telephone invitation to have lunch.

Verity flounces in to meet us, looking sober and lovely: she wears a flowing, silver-grey dress and has slung her hair into a chignon.

'Lovely hair, Mam' I say.

'My neck feels as bare and ready as Marie-Antoinette's,' she says.

Struan laughs and shakes her hand. 'You two could be sisters, honestly,' he says.

Verity grins like the newly mad, loving it, as usual, when someone makes that comparison, *plámásing* and all as it is. We are shown to our table and Struan helps Verity sit before pulling out my chair. We order drinks and Verity looks around the dining room, fingers the napkins and cutlery, then smiles at us both.

'Very nice, lovely,' she says, and turns to Struan, dipping her head in that seductive, little girl way she has. 'So, you're an arty hotelier? That'll be right up Lillis's street. Anthony, my ex-husband, is in education. Quite a gifted scientist.' Struan nods. 'But really, it's foolish to mix science with the arts, as we discovered.' She giggles, sips her tonic water, then turns to me. 'I hope our Lillis is behaving herself for you; she can be a handful.'

'Mam!'

'Oh, what? I'm only slagging, sweetheart. I'm sure Struan is well able for you.'

'Ready, willing and able,' Struan says, smiling across at me.

I start to wish I could leave the two of them to get on with their little pleasantries-fest by themselves. Smiling back at Struan, I place his hand on my knee under the table.

'Lovely,' my mother says again, to no one at all.

'Lillis has been telling me about your art works, Verity. They sound wonderful; I'd love to see some of them.'

'Oh yes?' Struan's hand lies on the table; Verity reaches across and touches his wrist. 'We can slip down to the Rubicon after lunch and you can view them there, if you like. Bronagh, my dealer, always likes to have several of my pieces in stock.'

Struan looks at me and, though it means we will be spending more of the day than planned with my mother, I nod and push out a smile.

'Yeah, great,' I say, 'let's do that. Verity, Struan has a gallery in the Strathcorry Inn, you know. It's fab. There have been some great shows.'

Verity nods. 'Really?'

The two of them bend over their menus and swap ideas about the food and about art; Verity acts coy and bossy, as she always does around men, and Struan, I can tell, is beguiled. They are enjoying their banter and the restaurant's elegance so much that I let them choose a soup and a fish dish for me. I don't even say anything when Struan orders a bottle of champagne, though I had warned him not to fill Verity with drink. I reckon a glass or two won't send her off and I am right — she is fine.

The overnight mist has thinned the air and I can hear an aeroplane flying overhead; its long, lonely drone makes me think of foreign things: equatorial heat, pale buildings, large over-crowded squares and an emerald sea. Listening to it makes me glad that I am leaving Dublin again for Scotland. I kick my feet into the cooler parts of the bed, then tuck them back under me. The whole hotel room is dull from the fog outside, which came down fast as we made our way back late through the city streets. The ceiling and walls and coverlet all shine, as if fighting against the grey. It reminds me, somehow, of the childhood excitement of waking to the luminescent light in my bedroom that meant new snowfall in the garden. Verity used to hunt me and Robin out of bed, so that we would be the first children in the neighbourhood to walk through the virgin snow. She loved the first snow of winter as

82

much as we did and it makes me happy to remember how good she could be at times.

My mind is too full to be tired; I pull the covers up over my head and try to force myself to sleep by imagining swathes of white paper rolling to a blank horizon. Acres of plain, unpainted paper have always been my substitute for sheep counting. But the image of all those white sheets starts me thinking of snow and then clouds and, soon, aeroplanes and holidays and the journey back to the Highlands. I toss my body sideways and attempt to will myself into tiredness.

'Stop wiggling,' Struan says, his eyes still closed.

'I can't.'

'Sleep is so beautiful; you should get more of it.'

'I would if I could. Something about being here makes me restless.' I cup my hand over Struan's cheek; it fits in my palm as snug and firm as an egg. 'Do you want to have a little hot fun?'

Struan groans. 'I'm wrecked, Lil.'

'OK,' I say.

I slip from the bed and go to the bathroom. I fill the bath to overfull and lie there in the steam, listening to the gurgle-urgle of the water in the outflow. Struan comes in, sleepy-eyed, and pees a long, slow stream into the loo.

'How can one man hold so much piss?' he says. He flushes and sits on the toilet seat. He scoops a handful of water from the bath and throws it over his face, slapping his cheeks and shivering. Bending towards me, he reaches into the bath and takes my hand. 'Lil, what would you feel about running the gallery at the inn when we go back?'

'What?' I sit up and my breasts bob on the water. 'Really?'

He kneels beside the bath and runs his hand up my abdomen. 'You're not going to win any awards for waitressing and I'm run ragged with everything else. You could make something of the gallery. What do you think?'

'I'd love it; I would just *love* it.' I kiss him and he climbs into the bath and lies on top of me, sending waves of water slooshing over the sides.

We arrange to meet Robin and Verity on O'Connell Street, to walk to the café owned by Robin's friend Fidelma, for dinner. We watch Robin teeter up on his bike. A bus blows its horn long and loud behind him; he humps off the saddle and wheels the bike beside the footpath, looking back at the driver who is balling his fist at him. Robin grins and waves and the bus-driver gives him the two fingers. He chains the bike to the post of the glass reliquary that stands on a traffic island. Inside, behind the smudged panes, a heart-bleeding Jesus holds his hands aloft, as if he is directing the traffic. I have always liked the look of that Jesus: his russet robes, the neat beard and seaweedy hair. Robin instructs the statue to look after his bike and I stroll beside him for the short walk to Fidelma's place on Frederick Street; Verity and Struan walk behind us.

'They look like a couple,' Robin says, glancing back. 'What age is he?'

'Fifty-one.'

'Four years older than Anthony. Is that a bit Freudian?'

'Shut it, Rob.'

We pass a woman with a smashed-up face selling cherries from an old black pram at the bottom of Parnell Square. Struan stops and buys some; he and Verity eat them, their heads bent conspiratorially close, their fingers dipping in and out of the punnet together. Something leaps in my chest but I tamp it down.

Fidelma runs to open the door for us. '*Fáilte*. Welcome,' she says, kissing me on both cheeks.

She is a handsome woman with wide eyes and one of those Irish chins that makes her face look bottom heavy. Fidelma is second generation Irish – her parents had left for England in the fifties – and she says that she feels like an in-between person. Her speech is often macaronic – she likes to speak partly in English, partly in Irish – and she always laments the fact that people in Ireland don't use their own language every day. I find her boring and domineering, but Robin adores her. We file through her café like a gang of schoolchildren and she seats us at a table at the back. The smells are bacon-and-cabbagey and Struan is charmed by everything.

Robin nods at the ruby lamps on the tables. 'They make the place look like a brothel,' he says.

'I was going for broodily atmospheric, but knocking shop is even better,' Fidelma says, clapping Robin's back and laughing.

I sit between Fidelma and Verity over lunch. Robin and Struan sit opposite us, and Fidelma is so loud I can't hear what they are talking about. Robin laughs a lot and he tries to smother his laughter – he thinks it is excessive, that he is giving too much of himself to Struan. I know this because his eyes fill with suppressed tears and he wipes them away even as he begins to giggle again. This is something he has always done when he is entertained and I am glad of it because it means he likes Struan; it means he is being open to him, allowing him in.

Fidelma wants to know everything about the Strathcorry Inn and Scotland, and she asks if I have been over to the islands where they speak Gàidhlig. She is pleased to know that I have heard it being spoken around Kinlochbrack and that it features on the street signs. She asks Struan about the menu in the bistro at the inn and they swap moans about unreliable staff.

'Hey, enough of that. *I'm* staff,' I say.

'Speaking of which,' Struan says, raising his eyebrows at me. 'Do you want to tell them your news?'

'Oh, OK.' I turn to Verity. 'Struan has asked me to manage the hotel's gallery when I go back.'

'You?' she says.

'Yes, Mam. Me.'

'Sounds great, Lillis,' Robin says. 'Congrats. You could have an exhibition of Verity's taxidart.'

Verity grabs her Coke and sips it, not looking at me.

'Would you do that, Mam? Bring your stuff to Kinlochbrack?'

'I don't know. Bronagh might get pissed off if I go exhibiting somewhere else. I can't be running here, there and everywhere at the drop of a hat. How would I even get the stuff transported?'

'It's an opportunity, Verity,' Fidelma says. 'Go international!'

'I'll see,' Verity says, closing the subject.

The trees along the centre of O'Connell Street are heavy with white bulbs and a parked ambulance splatters its blue strobe across the pathway. A teenage girl is being stretchered into the back, while her friends hold each other up and cry.

'It's like Christmas with all the lights,' Struan says, and I tilt my face up to him and agree.

'Do you think she'll do it?'

'Verity? Definitely. She was teasing you; I could tell she was delighted with the idea.'

'I don't know – she wasn't exactly jumping up and down.'

'Your first show to curate and it will be your mother's work. It seems apt.'

'I just hope she behaves herself if she comes over to Kinlochbrack.'

The ambulance wails past, making a blue mask of Struan's face; he stops, pushes both his hands into my hair and kisses me on the forehead. 'She will.'

Chapter Eleven

'Oh look, Daddy's little helper.'

Sam stands in the doorway of the gallery, a long room off the Strathcorry's reception area. I am flicking a feather duster along the top of the picture rail.

'Excuse me?' I say.

She swings her body back and forth, holding onto the doorframe. 'You always look so taken aback when someone speaks to you, Lillis. Boo!'

'I didn't know you were there.' I turn away from her.

She snaps the light switch on and off, on-off, on-off; the bulbs clink and fizzle, sounding annoyed. 'This is cushy, eh? Fuck all to do.'

'I have plenty to do, Sam.'

She sniggers and sits on a chair by the door. 'The big advantage to bedding the boss is getting the nice job, the easy number.' She takes a cigarette from its packet. 'Did you hear I got a promotion too? I'm manager of the bistro now.'

'Congrats. Don't light that fag in here.'

Sam taps the cigarette off the box and swings one leg over the other; she waggles her tennis shoe on the end of her toe and watches me. I take hold of the sweeping brush and chase dust-and-hair balls from the corners, then glide it up and down the main floor; the brushing rhythm stills my annoyance a little. I love the smell in the gallery: that clean, butcher paper scent mixed with wood and the acidic smell of the lights. I flutter the brush around the legs of Sam's chair; she sucks her shoe back onto her foot and stands up.

'What do you see in him, a lassie like you?'

I stop and look at her. 'It's not really any of your business.'

'Let me guess. You're one of those who wants taking care of.'

'Sam, I'm busy. Do you mind?'

'I'd say the reasons you like Struan are the exact reasons I couldn't stay with him. Who needs an old man who pretends to be a young man? It's sad.' She pushes the cigarette back into its box and goes to the door. 'Cheerio. I'll leave you to your *work*.'

When she is gone, I bash the sweeping brush along the skirting boards, then toss it to the floor; it clatters and I kick it across the gallery where it crashes against the far wall.

I like my room in the staff house. It is tiny – a small white berth – and feels cosy. I have a slim bed, an open wardrobe, a sink, and the wall is dappled with postcards from home and here, as well as pictures of Robin, Verity, Dónal, Anthony and the two boys, Alex and Tim. The corridor outside my room can be noisy at night – the other staff having parties or coming in late from work, or from The Windhorse – but that doesn't bother me. Once the key is in my lock, I am safe to rest, dream, write letters home, and sleep.

I keep Dónal's picture tacked to the wall near my pillow, so that I see him last and first each day; I tip his nose and say 'Good morning, mister' and 'Good night'. It is a photograph I took of him, for my project. He was a natural study; he never got that closed-up awkwardness that so many people take on when a camera is pointed at them – a look I know I get myself. The photo is black and white; Dónal is looking sideways and down, his lips slightly parted; a shuck of hair flops over his forehead. Under the crewneck of his T-shirt, I can see the bump of the silver belcher he never took off; I used to wrap my fingers into that chain when he lay over me.

My photography tutor said once that every photograph is a lie. Not this one: this picture holds the truth of Dónal like no other I ever took of him. He was talking when I shot him – Dónal didn't like silence – and I would give anything now to hear exactly what it was he was saying. This is something I have mulled over a lot: what did we talk about? He spent hours and days in my bedsit, in my bed; we talked and

88

talked and talked, but what did we have to say? How did we have so *much* to say? I am fucked if I can remember and it galls me.

Today, a package arrived from Mrs Spain; it was sitting on the desk in the gallery when I went in this morning. It squatted there all day, book-shaped but spongy, and I eyed it, wondering what might be in it. I studied Mrs Spain's square handwriting; I poked at the string she had used to keep the brown paper in place, despite the yards of Sellotape she had also used. The stamps were a line of Valentine's Day ones, depicting the same heart-shaped hot-air balloon over and over, with the word love, love, love scrawled underneath.

Now, I sit on my bed, holding the package in my lap like a bomb, not wanting to undo its wrappings. I turn to Dónal's picture, to his distracted, intent face.

'What's in the parcel, Dó?' I say. 'Will I open it?'

It is hard to look regal stepping off a diesel-belching bus, but Verity manages it; she holds herself erect, like someone who is aware they are important. Her legs are encased in long, red boots and she is done up in the make-up of her youth, as always: thick eyeliner, crumbling mascara and that odd shade of brown she wears on her lips. Verity hates villages and, she says, the sea gives her hives, but still she has come. Struan couldn't get away from the inn to go down to Inverness and pick her up, so she took a coach and now here she is, entering Kinlochbrack like a returning queen. I am among a huddle waiting on the pier for the bus; I stand on tiptoe and wave over the others' heads so she will see me. Verity walks forward with her arms held out, parting the crowd, and hugs me – her usual brittle, reluctant embrace. She stands back and holds me by the arms.

'You look well,' she says, then grabs me to her again.

I realise I have been pinching my mouth and nose shut, afraid to breathe her in, in case I smell drink. But I bury my face into her hair and smell nothing but the proper Verity smell: patchouli oil and, faintly, sweat.

'It's brilliant you're here, Mam,' I say, dragging her bag from the depths of the bus and steering her towards Shore Street. She stops to look around: at the sea loch, the boats, the hills, and the shops and pubs that overlook the water.

'It's a little idyll,' she says. 'Well done you.'

'We have a room ready for you at the inn. It's the best one – you can see Loch Brack from the window.'

'Let's look at this gallery of yours first,' she says, linking me as we walk. 'I have presents. Robin made me bring a six-pack of Tayto for you and your Dad sent a few bob; imaginative as ever. Is Struan still busy?'

'The hotel is manic just now. More staff have left; a couple of the Aussies took off to see Europe, so he's up to his eyeballs. He's reserved a table in the bistro and he'll join us for dinner later.'

Verity flips her head from left to right; she watches the traffic, the ambling tourists, the whole life of Kinlochbrack moving past us. She sucks in the sea-and-fish scent of the village.

'It makes me happy to shake the dust of Dublin off my feet,' she says. 'I'm all excited. I can't remember the last time I stayed in a hotel.'

'Wait until you see it – you'll love it.'

I feel a pang; it is great that she is giddy as a girl, but it makes me realise that she hardly leaves her home. Tom whizzes past in his vanette as we stand, waiting to cross the road; he beeps the horn and waves. I wave back; I can see him breaking his neck to get a look at Verity.

'Who was that?'

'Tom – the guy who delivers the bread. He's a friend of Struan's.'

Someone shouts, 'Hey, Lillis.' I see Kenny heading towards the pier and his boat, one hand raised in salute.

'How's it going, Kenny?'

'You've built a whole community here,' Verity says. 'What happened to my shy-as-a-badger Lillis?'

'I'm still me, Mam.'

We walk past the staff house and I point out the window to my room. The low clutter of buildings that make-up the Strathcorry Inn lies ahead and Verity surveys it all in silence, taking in the rose bushes and shrubs around the doorway and the dormer windows above it.

'Pretty,' she says.

Her good humour seems to be building, but I have long learnt to be frightened by Verity's happy moods because they are so likely to be temporary – an untrustworthy blip in her customary chaos. We slip through the reception at the inn, into the gallery.

'Here we are,' I say, standing back to let her walk the room.

She runs her hands along the white walls.

'Have you got all the plinths?' she asks, as she checks the lights.

'We have these three but I ordered more; they'll be here in the morning.' I point at the bulbs. 'Low-watt halogens; I bought them myself.'

She nods and proclaims the space big and bright enough, and I am relieved to have her blessing. I haul her suitcase up the stairs and deposit her in the low-ceilinged room that Struan has allotted her. It has a seaman's chest as a window seat, kilims on the floor and a dumpy four-poster bed. The room is quiet; it seems to hover above the concerns of the inn and the village; even the sea doesn't encroach. Verity pokes at the curtains and inspects the bathroom; she keeps her face neutral and there are no criticisms, so I know she is pleased. She wheels her case into one corner and says she will unpack later; we lie down on the bed, side by side.

'I love an adventure,' she says, and I take her hand in mine and squeeze it.

'Everyone loves Lillis,' Struan says.

'Not everyone,' I say, cutting into my steak to watch its pink ooze. 'There's Sam.'

Verity stops eating and waves her knife. 'Beauty bestows a fake consequence, you see, Struan. Good-looking women are always liked. By men, at least.' She lifts her hair from her neck with one hand. 'Is Sam that charming waitress?'

I snort. 'She's far from charming. Snotty bitch, more like.'

'Sam manages the bistro for me,' Struan says.

I am not failing to pick up on Verity's insinuation that all I have going for me are my looks, but she is in show-off mode and enjoying herself, so I let it go. Struan is bewitched by her and he laps up her words; he has the look of someone who has bought something expensive and finds himself extraordinarily pleased with the transaction. Struan and Verity are the same age, more or less, and I can see their generational ease with each other; that unspoken, added understanding shared by people who are born into the same time.

Verity grabs my hand across the table, but addresses herself to Struan. 'I do wish Lillis would lose that worried look she always has.'

'It's an Irish thing, isn't it? A kind of bashfulness.' He grins at me.

Verity smiles at no one in particular and runs her fish knife along the top of her sole, from head to tail.

'So, Struan, you're a Glaswegian. Why the wilds of Kinlochbrack?'

'My mother's mother was from The Braes, just above Kinlochbrack – Hannah Munro was her name. I toddled up here to the Highlands to see where she came from and stayed. This place pulls on people like that.'

'Ah, so you're a Highlander at heart.'

'He has the Highland work ethic, anyway – double- and triple-jobbing,' I say.

'Talk about hard workers, my Granny Hannah was some woman – a crofter's daughter turned glamour puss; she ran her own hair salon in Glasgow. I was crazy about her. My grandad was a bad egg, though, he gave her hell.'

Verity nods sympathetically. 'You have to go into the earth, explore and come out again to understand your parents, your whole family, your home. It's like *Alice in Wonderland*, isn't it?'

'Absolutely. And we can't call many places home – two maybe: where we spring from and where we eventually land. I call Kinlochbrack home; I'm happy here.'

Verity grins in my direction, as if this is somehow relevant to me. I am still pondering the *Alice in Wonderland* reference. I had asked her for that book as a child, only to be told I couldn't have it because it was 'a load of bloody nonsense written by a pervert'. I kept the word pervert rattling around in my head for years, mulling it over, until I finally found out what it meant. It left me with an unfounded distaste for Alice and her underground activities.

'The inn is lovely, Struan,' Verity says. 'Full of gorgeous things. Us Yourells are a family of object lovers, we love *things*.' She sips from her glass. 'Maybe more than we love people.' She hoots a laugh and grabs at my arm to let me know that this is meant as a joke. I want to say, 'But you don't love so much as plunder' but, of course, I don't.

Sam has been loitering near our table, waiting for a break in the conversation so she can step forward; Struan nods at her now.

'How are we all?' she says. 'Is everything OK?' She smiles, looking genuinely pleasant.

'Grand, everything is grand,' I say, and I see her wince.

'Mrs Yourell? Are you enjoying your sole?'

'It's absolutely perfect, sweetheart. You tell the chef he is a genius.'

'She – the Strathcorry's chef is a woman,' Struan says.

'All the better,' Verity replies, and holds her glass aloft. 'To Madame Chef.'

We clink glasses and Sam retreats. I am worried that Verity is going to be footless; her eyes are starting to wander in their sockets and she is repeating herself and doing the small sighs that mean her brain is getting fuddled. This is the point where things could go either way: she will stay nice, and chat sweetly, or she will soon get ratty about something innocuous or innocent that somebody says. Probably me.

'Are you tired, Mam? You've had such a long day. Would you like to go to bed?'

She swings in her chair to look at me, as if she has only just noticed I am there. I can see her making choices: will she accuse me of trying to get rid of her? Will she let it go?

'I'm fine, Lillis,' she says eventually, then turns back to Struan and smiles. 'Where were we?'

'Let's order dessert,' he says, jumping from his seat to get the menus.

Verity carefully scrapes lavender ice-cream from the bottom of a glass goblet; her concentration is immense and she doesn't speak; her eyes follow the last bits of ice-cream from the bowl to her mouth. She lays down her spoon and looks at Struan.

'Scotland is perfect. I have decided,' she says.

Struan laughs. 'We like to think so.'

'There's too much Ireland in Ireland, you know? It's all soggy and gummed up, with rain and the church and subterfuge.' Verity sighs and closes her eyes. 'Ireland is not emerald-shaped or harp-shaped or shamrock-shaped. It's de Valera-shaped. Fucked up and rotten. But still, I love it. I fucking hate the place, but I love it.' She sways in her seat. 'How can that be?'

'Bed now, Mam,' I say, patting her hand. 'Time for beddy-bye-byes.' It is always a risk using the softly-softly approach with Verity; she takes offence so easily. When she is prone to contrariness, I often want to batter her or throw a tantrum to match one of hers. But what would be the point? She is like a pre-pubescent girl sometimes, incapable of learning.

'What's that, Lillis?' she says.

'Bedtime. You've had a long, full day.'

She tries to focus on me and realises she can't, so she nods, pulls at her mouth with her napkin, then places it onto the table with care. I lean forward, kiss Struan on the lips and tell him I will be back shortly. I take Verity's elbow; she waves absently at Struan and I guide her up the stairs. Once in her room, I put her sitting on the bed; she lies down and sighs.

'You look like you're wearing widow's weeds,' she says, thrashing her hand at my black dress.

'I like it.' I smooth down the nap of the sleeves, hug myself with both arms. Verity is snoring lightly. 'Come on, Mam. We need to get you out of those things.'

She doesn't move. I undo her shoes, peel off her tights and skirt, and hoosh the covers over her. I shake out the tights, then hold them up to look at them; Verity's foot shape hangs inside the bottom of both legs, gullying them out like ghost feet, about to walk away. I fold the tights and her skirt, and place them on the sea chest. In a ritual from my childhood and teens, I put on the lamp, leave a glass of water and some tissues on the bedside table, and open the window a crack.

'I'll leave you now.'

'I'm glad I came. But I think I'll remain sober for the rest of my stay – less room for error that way.' Verity murmurs the words through the sheet she has pulled up to her nose.

'That might be an idea. Goodnight, Mam'

'Night, night, Lilybelle. Be good.'

I close her door quietly and stand on the landing, looking down into the stairwell; I can hear the faint clink-clank of dishes and glasses from the bistro, the low burble of piped music. Be good, Verity says, one of her mantras. *Be good.* How many thousand times have I heard those words from my mother? *Be good. Be good. Be good.*

'I am good,' I say, into the darkness, 'you just choose never to notice.'

A door opens further along and a couple come out into the corridor, laughing; I turn from Verity's bedroom door, put my hand on the banister and walk down the stairs to where Struan sits waiting for me.

Chapter Twelve

When I think of Dónal, I imagine the warm smell of skin, his tongue hot with the tang of beer, and him walking towards me through the city, cool under a sweep of ochre leaves. In my mind, Dónal is all about late autumn: gelid air, snug jackets and early-dark nights. I skitter backwards and remember his wide, little-boy smile as he sallied along, never in a hurry.

Some days he would turn up to meet me after my photography course or work – it was never pre-arranged – and we would walk a crowded Westmoreland Street or up Grafton Street, Dónal taking my hand. I would rub the rough pads of his long fingers while we strolled and talked. I looked into his face, liking the jag of his cheekbones and the way he tossed his head to chase the fringe out of his eyes. He was the type of boy that made everything not as it was. Dónal carried an air of impending excitement about him, and being with him meant a feeling of suspension in anticipatory moments. We walked Dublin without direction and sometimes we would end up by the quay wall in the dark, smelling the river.

'I'd hate to fall in there,' Dónal said once. 'I have a morbid fear of dying suddenly. Dramatically, you know?'

I hugged him from behind, my arms tucked around his waist, gently nosing the tobacco smell of his hair.

'Mmm,' I said, peering into the black churn of the water.

I turned him around to face me and pressed his back into the river wall; I took his cheeks in my hands and pushed my tongue between his lips. He tasted of the barley sugar sweets he sucked after each carefully smoked cigarette.

I remember the first time we tried to have sex; we had made a pact to practise together, the way youngsters do. We had already spent a couple of years perfecting our kissing on each other. I sat on the draining board; Dónal stood between my legs, his hands resting on my waist. My dress was pushed up on my thighs; I fiddled with the hairs on the back of his neck and looked over his shoulder at the clock.

'Half three. Verity will be back around five,' I said.

I stared at the stuffed rooster perched on a shelf, his beak a full grin of sharp teeth, his comb mottled and stiff. He wore a mossy tweed waistcoat. I was bothered that day; Verity had been drinking in the mornings – I could see it on her. She was fidgety and tense in the evenings; mellower during the day.

Dónal's hands slid up my thighs and he hooked one finger inside the leg elastic of my knickers, tickling at the hairs beneath. I looked straight into his eyes.

'Not here,' I said, sliding off the sink.

'OK.'

I pulled him from the kitchen through the sitting room, where Verity's dog lay on the sofa, showing her flabby underbelly with its spattering of mauve teats. When the dog walked, her belly swung in a way that I hated.

'Get off the sofa, Maxine.'

The dog looked up then turned her head away lazily; I poked at her with my boot, said, 'Stupid dog', and left her where she was. Dónal followed me up the steep stairs, into my bedroom. Verity used one corner of my room as a dump: perched in a heap were two broken chairs, piles of old magazines, a roll of chicken wire and a skew-eyed, stuffed squirrel. The heat of the house gathered in a fug in my room, under the pitched roof and, apart from my mother's mess, I loved it in there.

I sat on a pile of *National Geographic* magazines. Dónal knelt in front of me, the floorboards surely denting his knees. He slipped his hands under my skirt again and I slid forward for him. I pushed my nose into his damp neck and breathed on the smell of his unwashed skin. Pushing my feet into the floor, my toes slid inside my boots, while his fingers fumbled and poked. Dónal's breath was hot on my ear and I examined my fingernails behind his back: they were ridged and split, waiting to be picked at. A thin, dark line curved under each nail; later I would have a bath and watch the dirt loosen and float away. Dónal stopped his churning between my legs and kissed sloppily at my neck.

'Why don't we get into the bed?' Dónal said.

'All right.'

We lay down and I pulled off my knickers. Dónal slipped his jeans to his knees and yanked down his boxers. He climbed on top of me and kissed my neck some more.

'Is this OK?' he said, trying unsuccessfully to penetrate me, with short, sharp stabs. It hurt and I was pinned down and uncomfortable. I felt raw and annoyed and, after a while, I pushed him away, wiping at the slather he had left on my neck.

'What's wrong?' he said, pulling at his jeans; he tilted his head to look into my eyes.

'I think I heard Verity come in.'

'OK.' Dónal stood up. We fixed our clothes and trotted down the stairs.

'Hi, Lil, I didn't know you were here.' Verity looked up at us, then back at Maxine who lay beside her on the sofa; she stroked the dog and crooned into her face. Maxine's head was thrown back, her gums set in an ecstatic leer.

'You're back early, aren't you?'

'Will you stay to dinner, Dónal? I'm making a vegetable satay,' Verity said.

Dónal glanced at me. 'Sure.'

'You set the table,' Verity said to me, and stood up. 'Dónal can help me chop.'

In the kitchen, I watched my mother: she and Dónal were the same height, so when they turned to talk to each other, their noses nearly met. Verity asked Dónal how he was enjoying his mechanics course.

'Ah, it's grand. Something to do.'

'So, have you learnt anything?' I watched Verity lean towards him, her eyebrows questioning neatly.

'A few things, I suppose.' Dónal smiled at Verity, his eyes locked onto hers; it was the same look he gave me. Even the intimate, casual way he talked with my mother was the way he talked with me. I coughed; they turned away from each other and looked over.

'Are you all right there, sweetheart?'

'I'm fine.' I fiddled with a fork. 'You never ask me about my course.'

Verity turned back to Dónal. 'I'm having a party on Friday night, Dónal: a few people, some music. You should come. Tell your parents. And Cormac.'

I snorted. 'Cans of Tuborg and a plate of Scotch eggs for a load of ancient hippies does not constitute a party.'

'Ignore her,' Verity said, 'she's mad with me for loving life. *And* for leaving her father.' She laughed.

'I think you'll find that he left you, Mother. And, actually, it's your drinking that pisses me off.'

Dónal frowned. 'I'm going away this weekend with the lads.'

'You never said.' I knew I had no right to make demands when I wouldn't commit to anything more than the casual thing we had, but I was put out that he hadn't told me.

'Maybe I'll stay,' he said. 'I'll see.'

I wore one of my mother's cotton kaftans for the party: it had a pattern of brown and red swirls and it smelt of camphor. I pinched my hair up with a Spanish comb.

'Wow, you look gorgeous,' Dónal said, when I let him in. He pulled me into his arms to kiss me.

'There's no one here yet,' I said, pulling away from him to open the sitting room door.

Maxine ran to Dónal, sniffed his fingers and started to lick them; he bent down and rubbed her back.

'Hello Maxine, there's a good girl,' he said.

'Jesus, that dog. Come on, Max, there's no party for you, I'm afraid.' I crooked my finger under her collar and pull-pushed her out the door.

Dónal sat down and looked around. 'Cool', he said.

A fresh menagerie of stuffed animals stood around the walls, moved in from Verity's studio for the party: there was a faded wolfhound, two dinner-jacketed cats, a sneering fox – all of them draped in fairy lights and plastic flowers. The window sills held glasses and cutlery, paper plates and napkins. Verity leapt through the door, her hair wet and her cheeks red.

'My God, I'm a disaster. What time is it? Hello, Dónal, welcome, welcome, welcome.' She waved her arms. 'Where's Robin? Is he bringing the beer up from the shed? Lillis, are you watching the oven?'

Dónal stood up. 'Look, you go and finish getting ready, Mrs Yourell, and I'll check on things in the kitchen.'

'Oh, you're a honey.' She squeezed Dónal's arm. 'We'll keep you.' She winked at me and ran out of the room.

We went into the kitchen; it smelt of spices and garlic. Robin was sitting at the table smoking.

'Help me carry the beer from the shed,' he said to Dónal.

They left through the back door, chatting, and I started to feel I might enjoy the night. As long as Verity didn't get too drunk and start picking on me or, worse, tell stories about how grumpy I was as a child. Or show the photo of me as a three-year-old on a Galway beach, with the solid hump of a fresh poo visible in my knickers.

Guests began to arrive – a mish-mash of neighbours, Verity's friends, Robin's and a few of mine – and the house filled with smoke and chatter. A couple with guitars, old college pals of Verity's, set themselves up in a corner of the sitting room and started to play. Dónal rolled his eyes and asked the guitar player if he knew any Depeche Mode songs. I laughed and wandered around the sitting room, offering bowls of crisps and refilling glasses. I stopped beside my mother to listen to the guitar player mangle 'Hey Jude'.

Verity leaned into my side and handed me a can of lager. 'Robin has hit it off with that chap,' she said, nodding in the direction of Marcus, one of my course mates.

I took the drink, nodded and smiled, glad that Robin had found someone to chat to. He could be so awkward sometimes: either giddy or sullen, with no in-between mood. I went over to where Dónal was sitting side by side on the sofa with Audrey. I knew she fancied him, so I sat on Dónal's lap and swung my face into his.

'Kiss me,' I said, and Dónal gave me a peck on the lips. I grabbed his cheeks in my hands and kissed him deeply. 'Like that,' I said.

'You're drunk, Lillis,' Dónal said, and heaved me off his knees. He grinned at Audrey, who laughed; I stood and stared at them.

'I'm not drunk. This is my first drink.' I waved the can of beer at him. Dónal shrugged, then looked over at Audrey and they both cackled. I bent down low to them. 'Fuck the two of you,' I whispered, and walked away.

I went into the kitchen and threw patéd crackers and dishes of mini pretzels onto a tray and offered them around. When I got back to the sitting room Dónal and Audrey were gone. A man said I looked just like my mother at the same age. I smiled and linked Verity; we listened to the singing. When the musicians took a break, I ate five cocktail sausages, one after the other, then went to find Dónal. I pushed through the crowds in the kitchen but couldn't see him. Straggles of guests were gathered in the garden and I walked among them, looking for Dónal's familiar shape. I shoved open the shed door but there was no one there.

'Looking for someone?'

I turned to see Dónal sprawled on the grass, smoking a joint with his brother; I hadn't seen Cormac arrive.

'There you are,' I said.

Dónal giggled. I ruffled his hair with my fingers. 'You need a haircut, Redser.'

'Here, have a toke on this; it's great stuff.'

'Don't give that to her,' Cormac said, 'she's too young.' He snapped the joint from Dónal's hand.

'I'm the same age as him,' I said.

'Exactly,' Cormac said. 'Don't smoke it, Lillis, it'll make you sick.'

I took the joint from Cormac and dragged off it; the smoke hit the back of my throat like a punch and I sucked it in and held it, as I had seen others do. I laughed the smoke out.

'Jesus, that tastes weird.'

'Don't go getting used to it,' Cormac said, and winked at me.

I felt my whole head blush. I sat on the grass beside them and Dónal squinched up behind me and put his arms around my waist.

Chapter Thirteen

Verity hacks through a crescent of honeydew melon at breakfast in the bistro; its mint green flesh and spilling seeds seem to be getting the better of her.

'Do you want a hand with that?'

'No. I'm not even hungry.'

She throws down her spoon and fork. Her eyes are pink-shot and she looks close to tears; for a while she kept up the frivolous, eager-to-please banter that always accompanies her hangover, but she has finally slumped.

'It will be good to get the work into place in the gallery – Struan says the crates arrived from Dublin early this morning.'

Verity shudders and pulls on her cardigan. 'Lots of work to do then.'

'The art critic from *Scotland on Sunday* is coming up from Edinburgh for the opening. I rang him.'

'Fucking journalists; most of them wouldn't know a bee from a bull's foot.'

'Well, this guy seems nice and he writes books as well, so he might have a clue.'

'We'll see,' she says, a phrase I hated to hear from her as a child, because it could mean something positive or something negative, or simply nothing at all.

The gallery is higgledy-piggledy with wooden Artex crates that spew foam peanuts and skeins of plastic wrapper. Verity is moving the plinths like a titan.

'Would you please leave them until Struan comes?'

'Shush.'

Her artworks stand against one wall; most of them are new pieces that she has completed since my trip to Dublin. There is a pirouetting white mouse, balanced on the head of a pin, under a bell jar; a goat kid with a unicorn's horn and wings, toting a cowboy pistol; and a pigeon in a cobalt ball gown, with matching eyes, who bears an alarming resemblance to my prim – and dead – Granny Yourell.

'This is clearly mother-in-law revenge,' I say. 'She even has Granny's cigarette holder.'

Verity giggles. 'Good, isn't she? I call her The Bower Bitch; bowers love anything blue.'

'I just hope she doesn't start talking: "Lill-*iss*, why is your face so dirty? Lill-*iss*, you are so unwomanly, why aren't you wearing a dress? You are a bold girleen, Lillis Yourell, you make our Blessed Lady cry." '

We both laugh and Verity wanders away, sizing up the positions of the plinths. I plunge my hand into one of the crates, pluck the curly peanuts between my fingers, pull them out of the box, into the air, and let them fall. I hum to myself, pushing my hands in deep again, enjoying the tickle of the packing stuff on my skin. I don't hear Verity behind me until I sense the swish of her palm passing my ear; she slaps me on the side of my neck.

'Stop messing, Lillis.'

'Jesus, Mam – that hurt.' I put my hand on the spot she hit.

'No, it did *not* hurt. Help me set up this corner; I want The Unicorn Kid over here.'

'Well, you gave me a fright; I didn't know you were behind me.'

'Stop being a pain. Are you going to help me or not?' Verity says.

'I will help. I am helping. This is my *work*, for God's sake. This is what I do.'

'Well get to it then,' she shouts, flicking a scarf of plastic wrap at my face.

It scratches across my cheek before catching in my earring. At the same moment, Struan comes through the gallery door. Verity knows she is caught when he stands looking at the pair of us: her wide-eyed and stock still, me unhitching the plastic from my earring and wincing in pain. When I get it free, I throw up my hands to show Struan what I mean about my mother's mercurial behaviour.

'Everything OK?' he says.

I brush past Struan to get to the door. 'This is the softly done mania she excels at.'

He grabs my wrist. 'Don't go. Sort this out now, come on.'

I pull my arm out of his grip and glare at him. 'Excuse me,' I say, and walk out into the inn's reception.

'She gives me the pip,' I hear Verity say to Struan; I don't wait to hear if he replies.

I watch the shudder and swell of the dancers under the lights – girls and boys, women and men. They plough and weave together, lost inside their own bodies. The music beats through my chest and thumps against my heart. Boom-thump-boom-thump-thump-thump. *Everybody dance now*, the singer screeches. It is one of my favourite tracks to dance to, but I stay in my seat and follow the sway of a hundred bodies with my eyes. The hall looks festive; it is strung with garlands of lights and a mirror ball flickers diamonds of white across the dancers' heads and the walls.

I see Struan before he sees me; he hems the edge of the dance floor, looks into the crowd and stops to greet people as he goes. He has his arm around Kenny's neck, mock strangling him, when he spots me. He raises one hand, then does a hip boogie to make me laugh. I turn away and slug my pint.

'Not dancing, Lil?' Struan, beside me now, shouts above the music.

'Nah. Just drinking.'

'Like mother, like daughter.'

'Fuck off.'

The music slows down and the dance floor clears. 'Come on,' he says, 'give me your paw.'

I stand up, take his hand and he swirls me around and bows, before holding me as if we are going to waltz. I put my arms around his neck. We sway to the music and I try to find somewhere to put my eyes. I don't want to look at Struan, but neither do I want to catch the gaze of the couples who are lurching earnestly around us.

'Where is Verity?'

'She's gone to bed. The exhibition is all set up.'

Struan pulls me forward so that our pelvises meet; he tightens his hands to the small of my back. He dips his head to my ear and sings along to the song we are dancing to, asking me how he's supposed to live without me.

I laugh. 'Shut up, will you?' The song ends and we walk hand in hand back to my seat. I swallow the last of my pint; it tastes like soap bubbles. 'Let's go; I've had enough.'

It is cold outside the hall. The village and harbour sit below us; there are boats dotted in the loch which shines like quicksilver and the streetlamps throw tentacles of orange onto the water. Struan wraps his arm around my shoulders and we start the descent down the tarmac road into Kinlochbrack.

'Your mother might be a pain sometimes, but she's only here for a few days. Stop acting like a brat and spend some proper time with her.'

'She annoys the shite out of me; she hit me, you know.'

'I saw it.'

'No, before that. She snuck up behind me and slapped me across the neck.'

'She's nervous about the show, I suppose; she's on edge.'

'Will you stop defending her? She was hungover today, end of story. She gives me a pain in my hole.'

'That's what mothers do. First and foremost they are themselves, and that won't change. And they have their own vision of things, of how their kids should be and act and react and it doesn't match our vision for ourselves. Be nice to her.'

'Verity makes it so hard. One minute she's grand, the next she's lashing out like a psycho.'

'Try to be patient.'

'I will, I will. I'll make it up to her tomorrow.'

He hugs my shoulder into his side and, with his free hand, lights a cigarette.

Verity and I are dusting the bell jars and all the intimate folds and grooves on the uncovered pieces of art. I am using a badger hairbrush to clean in between the creases of the chimpanzee's pinny.

'Promise me you'll do this daily. Don't let any dust gather whatsoever,' she says.

'I promise.'

'I feel like I'm leaving my arms behind,' she says, biting down on her lip.

'You knew they would sell, that you'd have to part with them sometime.'

'They're so new; I've barely bonded with them and they're off.'

'You have money now for more materials. You'll be able to start lots of pieces the minute you get home.'

Verity grunts.

Struan bustles in, shaking a newspaper. 'Listen to this. Listen!'

Verity and I put down our brushes and turn to him.

'Go on,' she says, 'get it over with.'

'*Intelligent Surrealism at the Strathcorry Gallery. There is nothing passé about the artwork currently on display at Kinlochbrack's Strathcorry Gallery. Irish fine-art taxidermist Verity Yourell from Dublin calls herself a 'taxidartist' – a term, I must confess, that makes me cringe. Is she Ireland's only taxidartist, I enquire? Her reply is blustered and impatient: "Of course not. But I am the only one doing it right." I suggest that skinning and stuffing animals for a living is not a particularly feminine pursuit and am met with silence. Ms Yourell clearly does not agree. And why should she agree? As Ireland's best taxidartist she is flying the flag for all artists who choose to follow their own path. She then informs me that the pioneer of taxidermy, as we know it today, was an American woman named Martha Maxwell. "A lifelong vegetarian," Yourell states, lest I question Maxwell's credentials as an animal lover.*'

Struan pumps one hand through the air to emphasise the bits he likes, and glances at Verity to see how she is reacting. She stands with her eyes closed.

'*Nomenclature aside, Yourell's fantastical stuffed animals are a welcome injection of intelligent surrealism into the current art scene. I am particularly taken with a glamorous pigeon entitled* The Bower Bitch *– which the artist says is "one* *of the suicidal pigeons of Capel Street". She hit the bird – accidentally – with her car, and there was apparently "nothing for it but to take her home and re-birth her". The blue-gowned bird holds a tiny tortoiseshell and gold cigarette holder of such perfect proportions it's hard to know how it was fashioned.*

Yourell says that generally she acquires the animals free of charge and that mostly she doesn't take people's pets. "The owners expect their pets to look like they were when they were alive, and with me on the job," she waves her arm to indicate her artworks, "that's not going to happen." The artist states that the animals are chased into her life "by serendipity, the muse's busy twin."

If all art is an ironic attempt to perpetuate the self, then eyebrows will surely be raised at Yourell's vision of herself: she is at times a pirouetting mouse, at other times a pipe-smoking chimpanzee. The viewer is engaged, amused, perhaps even appalled at the animals' eccentric beauty. Taxidermy may be the dirty little secret of the world of fine art, but Verity Yourell is its shining beacon. The effect of her menagerie – tucked into a tiny Highland gallery, when surely the show deserves an Edinburgh or London outing – is stunning.

The works, despite being dead as dead, pulsate with a knowing wit and a life that puts Yourell's younger contemporaries to shame. She explores the potential of humans for folly through our animal brethren and she does so with charm and skill. And, just like her artworks, Verity Yourell is something of a maverick and, most definitely, a true original. Strathcorry Gallery, Kinlochbrack, until August 31st. What do you think of that?' Struan almost shouts the words.

'It'll be lining the bottoms of budgie cages by Friday,' Verity says.

'Now, Mam, that is what I call a glowing review,' I say, taking her hand.

She smiles, drags me into her arms and lets a squeal. Over my shoulder she beckons to Struan and he bounces across and puts his arms around both of us.

'Take it, Verity. It's brilliant, just brilliant,' he says.

'It is brilliant,' she says, and puts her head onto my shoulder. The three of us rock together in silence.

Chapter Fourteen

I sit on the harbour wall by Loch Brack and swing my legs over the water; it is flat calm and a seal raises its head out of the murk, its raisin eyes curious. I bite into a beef sandwich and look at the Klondyker ships hulking in the bay like the forgotten remnants of a war. They are battered and loaded with ragged nets; one ship even has a Lada on board, sitting white and impatient on the deck. It is a drowsy day but, behind me, The Windhorse is having a busy afternoon – drinkers scatter out through the door onto the footpath and huddle in groups. They call to each other in Russian and I realise they are workers on shore leave from the factory ships, free for a few hours from processing mackerel by the thousand. My sandwich is not agreeing with me – my stomach fizzles and aches – so I shove it back inside its wrapper and toss it into my satchel.

The sky over the loch is a peculiar zinc and tangerine; the sun beats on my face and shoulders, worms its way into my pores. I let the voices from the pub and the traffic noise fade; I enter one of those momentary contented highs that exist beyond life, beyond reality, in a sort of dream garden. I let myself linger in that trance, like someone who has passed into another world; I sit for a moment in that bliss, owning it, then I wander out again. These transcendent sparks don't happen a lot, but are so welcome when they do. There is a barn in a field on the road between Galway and Dublin, near Tyrrellspass. When I see that barn – every single time – I experience one of those golden moments. Depending on what season it is, the red barn sits on its slope above a field of glossy green barley; or muck ploughed into perfect ridges; or an eiderdown of snow. That barn, alone against the sky, pulls at my insides. It is perfect somehow, simple and elemental, like babyhood. I have never photographed it; I prefer to hold it in the pocket of my memory and be delighted by it every time I pass the field it lives in, on my way to or from my father's house.

A tap on my shoulder. 'Miss, would you like to buy cigarettes?' It is one of the Klondykers.

'No, thanks, I don't smoke.'

Struan has told me he wouldn't touch the fags they sell; they are cheap and stinking. The man reaches into his plastic holdall and pulls out a matryoshka doll. He hands it to me.

'She has many inside. Look.'

He makes twisting motions with his hands. I open the doll. She is nothing special: her yellow casing is painted with a red rose. She has four nesting sisters; the smallest one – a red, frowning peanut – doesn't match the others. The bigger dolls are pink cheeked and smiling. I have seen the same matryoshka for sale in gift shops in Dublin, but the man's earnest, needy eyes make me ask him how much.

'Ten pounds,' he says.

I hand back the doll. 'No thanks.'

'Eight.'

'Five,' I say.

'Nyet,' he says. Then, 'Uck.' It is part defeat, part exasperation; I see a line of gold teeth in his mouth. I hand him the money and he gives me the doll; I rattle her gently and put her into my satchel. The man nods and walks away.

The index finger on my right hand begins to itch; I examine the tiny red bump that has appeared there on and off over the years and scratch at it. It reminds me of the summer I tried hard to become a smoker; I never took to it because Dónal and Robin laughed so hard at my attempts to inhale that I felt like a fool; I backed away from the smoke, blinking, and held the cigarette at arm's length. Dónal called me a dope, so I gave up as soon as I started. The finger-bump had appeared then, like a memento mori to remind me that cigarettes don't suit me.

Dónal again. As ever present as my own blood. It doesn't take much to conjure him. I sling my bag across my body, hoosh myself off the sea wall and walk down a busy Shore Street. Back in my bedroom, I put the matryoshka on my windowsill and root in the wardrobe. I take out the package Dónal's mother sent. I sit on my bed and undo the string, the brown paper, the Sellotape. Inside, swathed in a wad of bubble wrap, is a photo album. With it, a note: 'Yours, I think. And if not yours, have it anyway. I hope all goes well in Scotland. Verity gave me your address. Sincerely, Treasa Spain.' In the album there are pictures of me from birth to age twenty. A lot of the photos were taken with Mr Spain's Instamatic, but a few of them were lifted from my parents' house. I haven't seen some of these pictures in years.

The pages are those sticky bump-lined ones and the pictures are held in place by plastic sheets. Under the plastic, I sit: a pudding-faced baby in a square pram; at age five in a school photo, a cold sore on my mouth subduing my smile. Me on my first Holy Communion day, veiled and smirking. (That one was taken from its frame on our sitting room mantelpiece and Robin had been blamed for destroying it out of jealousy. There was murder over it.) Here are Dónal and me having our wedding: a pillowcase dress and daisy garland for me; a school tie and tweed cap on Dónal; neither of us with any front teeth. Me, squinting into the lens at Dublin Zoo, giraffes swinging behind. Me drunk, waving a can of lager, eyes scrunched up to ward off the camera. Me paddling in the sea at Salthill, Black Head lurking like a behemoth in the background. Me sad-faced, me radiant. Me with stupidly short, puffy hair. Me with Dónal.

Some of the images make me laugh; some make me gasp at what the spoon of memory stirs up to go with them: the hot smell of animal shit at the zoo; the feel of dewy grass soaking through the back of my shorts; my mother's firm grip as she clipped the daisy garland into my hair, so like her own hair. How young she was.

I can't commit to one set of feelings about this album; this homage or obsession or whatever it is. Is it creepy? Is it lovely? I cannot settle on whether I feel violated, guilty, touched, annoyed or tender. I flick through its pages over and over – I haven't seen many of the pictures before; some explain the gaps in our family albums that annoyed my father so much. All of it explains Dónal. I sit on the bed and hug it to me; I rock with it, keening quietly for Dónal and all he could not and never will have. It takes less than nothing to make me cry these days.

I fall asleep with the album held to me and dream of Dónal. For once he is not distant or untouchable. He stands before me and I cup his face in my hands and tell him that I am sorry. He smiles and the dream skitters off in its own direction, barely taking me with it.

I know the exact day that it happened; it was the Saturday of the hike. Either up there on the hills above Kinlochbrack, or later that evening when I got mad drunk. I swilled wine like water that night and Struan half-carried me from The Windhorse to my room in the staff house. He meant to go back up to the inn, to wrap up the night, but I forced him to stay and we had sex on my little, narrow bed. I can barely remember it; I just know that we didn't use anything because I said to him afterwards, 'If I'm pregnant, I'll kill you.' I remember that. We hadn't used anything up on the brae either, but it didn't seem to matter to me then. No, for some reason when I was drunk, I cared – the weird moral clarity of the stocious.

Fuck. And now Robin is on his way to Kinlochbrack to see Verity's show and I will have to tell him or not tell him. If I don't say anything he will know something is up because I won't be able to go for drinks and he will be suspicious. And if I *do* tell him he will tell Verity and Anthony, because Robin can't hold his piss. I look at the matryoshka on my windowsill, her smaller selves sealed inside her; the tiniest one a foetus-like thing, snugged deep. Her expression looks self-righteous to me – smug. Oh fuck, fuck, fuck. What am I going to do? What in God's name would *I* do with a baby? I haven't the first notion about how to be a mother and I don't want to learn either. How did I miss the monthly need for sweet things that comes on as predictably as the bad mood that goes with it? This is wrong, all wrong.

I drop the pregnancy test into the bin; its twin lines wink like candy stripes, sweet and gentle harbingers of happiness. Taking the test back out, I wrap it in tissues and shove it right to the bottom of the bin. I leave my room and the staff house and walk to Margaret's place on Market Street.

'You poor wee thing,' Margaret says. We are sitting on opposite sofas in her lounge, drinking tea. 'It's such a tragedy.'

I look at her, clutching Charlie to her body though he squirms and tries to get away; she lifts and shifts him while he tenses his limbs against her movements. I find him repulsive suddenly, with his snot-sticky face and endless need for attention.

'A tragedy? How?'

'Well, pet, if you don't mean to tell Struan, I'm guessing you're going to have an abortion.' She spits the word.

'I don't know what I'm doing yet; I can't think straight. Should I go to a doctor, do you think?'

'Yes, pet, I can ring ours and get you an appointment. I'll sort that out, don't you worry.'

Behind her sincerity, I can see Margaret taking everything in, storing up my words and actions to relay to Gordon. They will chew over it all, digest the hard bits and try to figure it out. I know this without ever having heard myself dissected; I have seen them at work on others. Her earnest milk-heaviness sickens me now; her plumpy, all-woman perfection. Margaret is not yet thirty but she seems a thousand years from where I am. She puts Charlie to her breast, fumbles herself out of her bra and I watch the baby's greedy snuffling as he digs in.

I wish now that I had said nothing, that I hadn't told Margaret; I can't believe I blurted it out. All I wanted was to say it aloud, to test the sound of it. *I am pregnant.* I could have said it to myself in my bedroom, or shouted it down the beach to a passing gull. *I'm fucking pregnant!*

'I have to go,' I say, getting up. 'Promise me you won't tell Struan a thing.'

'I promise,' she says, her eyes, like a hurt dog's, reproaching me.

I am busy in the gallery, doing paperwork. This is my favourite time of the morning, before anyone comes in to view the exhibition, and before the inn has properly gotten going for the day. I can get on with things and not think about myself. I perch on my high stool at the shelf that I use as a desk, sorting through letters, mostly from artists who want to have an exhibition. Some send poor images of their work;

most don't even bother with that much. I hear footsteps at the door and glance idly up from the pile of envelopes and sheets of paper. A tall man stands there – lots of blonde curls, a silly goatee. I look away for a second, then leap from my stool and throw myself onto him.

'Rob! You're early! How are you early?' I hug Robin hugely and step back.

'You've put on weight,' he says, 'it suits you.'

'Really? Where?'

'Your face. Here,' he says, pinching my hips.

'That's a stupid beard,' I say. 'Coffee? Food? I'm starved.'

While we walk across reception to the bistro, he tells me that he stayed the night in Inverness and took the early bus up to Kinlochbrack. Struan is supervising breakfast and he grabs Robin's elbow with one arm and slaps him on the shoulder with his free hand.

'Well, you got here safe and sound. Lillis has a key – leave your stuff down to the house.'

'Thanks for the bunk.'

'No bother, man.'

Under a purpling sky, I watch rainclouds spread eastwards across Kinlochbrack. The Highlands have been rain bullied for thirteen days and this is the first dry spell. But the storm is on its way back and the grey of it oppresses me. I am dawdling in front of the draper's shop on Ardmair Street, examining a chipper-nippled mannequin with an impossibly flat stomach. The place is closed but the shopkeeper steps into the window and dresses the dummy in a wax jacket and nothing else. He disappears from view.

My own stomach feels swollen though, in truth, it looks the same as ever; I put both hands on my belly and swing this way and that to examine my reflection. There is no full-length mirror in the staff house or in Struan's. The window dresser reappears and plops a red tartan deerstalker on the dummy's head, wraps an orange pashmina around her throat then drapes it to cover her breasts. He looks at me and pulls a face, as if I am responsible for how daft his display skills are. I shrug and walk on; I slip into the church. The weekly Mass is underway; I sit at the rear of the church and the priest begins his homily. He exhorts the congregation not to be afraid of truth.

'Speak the truth to yourself and to others. Always,' he says. 'Try it out. You might like it.' A few titters. 'If truth is rock, then sand is notions or feelings. Don't build your life on sand. I urge you to construct a life that honours truth, as Jesus did.'

My mind wanders. I examine the mournful statues, the stained glass spilling light like hope across the floor, in lozenges of blue and yellow. But all the time the word *truth* crashes into my consciousness as the priest continues his sermon. *Tell the truth. Don't build your life on sand. Honour truth.* I bless myself, genuflect and shuffle out of the pew. Once outside I turn my nose for Clanranald Street.

BOOK TWO: 2011

BOOK TWO: Self

Chapter One

I wake in the night, sweat-hot and stuffy headed, with a phrase dancing like a mantra through my mind: *The quick and the dead. The quick and the dead.* I sit up, sure that the baby is gone; that it is no more than a kidney-shaped blob, clinging by a fibre to the inner wall of my womb, its tiny heart stopped. Sobs bubble from my mouth – big, shuddering, ridiculous sobs – and tears slip down my face. *The quick and the dead. The quick and the dead.* When I realise I am howling – I hear the terrible sound of myself as if from another room – I clamp my lips tight, not wanting to wake Cormac. It all stops as fast as it started, but I am fully awake now; I look at Cormac, deep in sleep, and envy him. I reach for the pregnancy book that sits, bible-like, on the bedside locker.

Quickening, I read, *is the first faint fluttering movements of your baby at about eighteen weeks' gestation. It was once believed that the baby only became alive at this time.*

'Became alive,' I say aloud, and feel comforted. 'Become alive.' I pat my belly, rub it, and tell the baby to be good. 'Stay with me, please, stay,' I urge. I cannot lose another child.

The baby is slow to get going most days, preferring to loll about in the nest of my belly while I settle into the morning. I wait every day for it to wake. Cormac handles my bump each time he passes me. He loves to feel and see the baby move, making patterns under my skin, and he holds his palms against my tummy, cradling me like an anointing priest. When my bump is bared, Cormac kisses my mottled belly skin and says, 'This is your daddy. I'm here. I can't wait to meet you.'

The scans are more frequent now and when the doctor – while probing my swollen stomach with cold gel and her magic wand

– comments that the baby is lazy, I agree. We watch the screen and track the baby's liquid movements: the slow curl of a fist or waggle of the head. It is hard to believe that the fuzzy monochrome image is anything to do with the life that stirs under the mound of my stomach: it is like looking into outer space.

'You've no disco dancer there,' the doctor says, and gives me a chart to record the baby's every move.

'Your first?' the midwife says, wearing me like a glove puppet.

'Yes.'

She presses my knees wider apart and eyeballs me, not sure, I suppose, why I am lying. She withdraws her fingers with a suck.

'Five centimetres,' she says.

Cormac looks at me, then at her. 'This is our second baby, really. My wife had a miscarriage last year, at fourteen weeks.'

The midwife nods. 'Daddy, will you wait outside a minute?'

'I'll be in the corridor.' Cormac squeezes my hand; he leaves the room.

'Mrs Spain,' the midwife says, frowning at me, 'a stitched perineum heals eventually but, let me tell you this, it leaves a scar. And anyway the post-partum vulva never goes back to its former state. Are you with me?'

'What does it matter?' I hiss, bending into another contraction and humming my way through it.

'Please yourself,' she says, snapping off the white gloves that are brown with my blood. 'Was it a difficult birth?'

'Forceps.'

'When?'

'Twenty years ago.'

'This one will come easier.' She smiles tightly and opens the door with her foot. 'Daddy Spain,' she calls, and Cormac comes back in. 'Five centimetres means we're halfway there. Halfway to somewhere.' She leaves.

'Are you OK?'

'I'm grand. One's just ending. They're coming faster now.'

Cormac looks stricken, frightened. He rubs my arm. 'Will I text Verity? My ma?'

'Wait until the baby's here.'

Another contraction begins to band my belly; I start to hum again, pressing the noise into the roof of my mouth. I get to my knees and rock, holding onto the bed rail.

'Poor love.' Cormac stands to the side of the narrow bed and places one hand to the base of my spine. I push against him to ease some of it, to feel him there, solidly behind me. When the contraction subsides I collapse onto his arm. 'You're doing great, Lillis. You're brilliant.'

He helps me off the bed and I stand at the window, looking down at the street. A teenage boy cycles past, the front wheel of his bike wobbling while he uses one hand to pull a croissant from a paper bag and snatch bites from it. I can see the railings of Merrion Square Park and I think of the statue of Oscar Wilde that is in there, slouched on a rock, leering stupidly. I sway from side to side, holding onto my belly. Another contraction starts and I grip the windowsill and close my eyes; I concentrate on the cold floor against the soles of my feet. A stray thought flies: if the baby is a boy, maybe we will call him Oscar.

'Oscar for a boy?' I say, as the pain descends and peters out.

'It's a girl, I can feel it in my waters.'

The labour gets too much; I start to weep and hiccup, I feel shivery. Nothing Cormac says comforts me. He pulls woolly socks over my toes and puts my dressing gown on my shoulders. I shrug him off when he tries to hold me. The midwife offers jabs and gas; I take the epidural. Just as I did last time.

Back then, a junior midwife from Edinburgh and I did crosswords and watched cookery programmes on a TV that was stuck high on the wall in that long-ago room. A blue room. A room the colour of forget-me-nots where my son was pincered from me and I tore open, in more ways than one. He emerged bloody, bruised and quiet, nosing the air like an expert, taking us all in: me, the young midwife, the consultant and his flock of medical students who were brought in to learn what a difficult birth looks like. They stood by my high bed and discussed what they had witnessed, while the young midwife hauled the placenta out of me and I held my son and shook. When all the tests were done and the room emptied out, we stepped through the sunrise together: me, the young midwife and my son. Fingers of rain pulled along the small window of the labour ward and we sat in the quiet, the three of us.

Now, I imagine my labia, first like the gluey, crenulated frill of a snail, easing backwards; then pulled taut when the baby's head juts against the opening, rushing forward to meet us. This is the most up-to-date epidural and with it I can feel the baby's progress down the canal; it is a positive sensation, a grounding to earth.

Cormac holds one of my knees, the grim midwife the other, and I push, chin to chest; push, push, push.

'That's it. Good girl,' the midwife says. 'You're a champion at this. Good girl, good girl.'

It is a long time since I have been called a good girl and it makes me giggle. Cormac looks at me and grins. 'Nearly there, love.'

I want to be present at both ends. I want to be the one pushing life into the world and I want to stand at the end of the bed, watching my child's head force through.

'Baby's nearly here, Mrs Spain. One big push now. Come on, let's go.' The midwife drops my leg and scurries to the foot of the bed. 'Here's the head.'

She grabs my hand and places it onto the wet, pulsing skull of my baby. 'Oh,' is all I can say, at the thrill of it, the velvet life of it. 'Oh!'

'Come on, now. Here we go.'

I push down with force and the baby whooshes out into the midwife's hands.

'Jesus,' Cormac shouts, 'it's a baby.' We all burst out laughing, me hysterically. Like the first time I gave birth, I am shaking and cannot stop.

'It's a girl,' the midwife says, and plops her onto my already slackening belly; her pickled beetroot skin is warm and soft. The baby nods her head as if to say, 'Yes, I have come. I am here at last.'

Before I gave birth, the young Edinburgh midwife offered me a sweet which I took, then another, which I refused, because I didn't want her to think of me as one of those people who takes everything that is on offer. She told me not to tell the other midwives that I had eaten a sweet because I was meant to be fasting. She was a gentle girl, eager to be pleasant – the way, I had found, many Scottish people were.

'Mum's the word,' I said, and we both laughed, a little awkwardly.

'Why are you giving up the baby?' she asked. 'You seem nice. Capable.'

I folded my hands over my bump. 'This is the last thing I'm cut out for. Bad mothers run in my family.'

'What does the dad think?'

I shook my head. 'He doesn't know.'

'Most girls would, you know, terminate.'

'I'm happy to give the baby to someone who really wants it. You know, a woman who can't get pregnant, or is too old, or whatever.'

'You're brave,' she said, rolling another sweet from the packet and popping it into her mouth.

'It would probably be braver to keep it,' I said.

We were left alone for an hour. Baby Malachy in his clear plastic cot, so like a tub; me on my bed, with tea and toast, gazing down on him.

The midwife returned.

'Baby has to leave now,' she said, as if he was going to take himself out of his cot and walk away across the floor.

Her words were hard to take in. My ears fended them off and pushed them away into the air. I stared at the midwife, feeling helpless and stranded on the delivery bed. My head was wobbling – actually shaking up and down – and the euphoria of finally getting to see the baby drained from me like sweat. It was a long, stubborn birth, all of me was empty and sore, but here he was, the boy who had made me huge, who had kicked me to pieces for months on end. The midwife put her hand on my arm and rubbed my skin, hurting me; I was too distracted to tell her to stop.

'Now? Does he have to go right now?'

'You should hold him again.'

She placed the bundle that was my son into my arms. My little Malachy. Malachy Dónal. His face was the colour of corned beef – he looked as if he had been boiled. He had a pug nose, tiny eyes and a pouting lower lip. I kissed him on his hot, soft cheek. Malachy was the most beautiful thing I had ever seen; he looked like neither me nor Struan but was a total person all to himself. I held his neck in my elbow crook and breathed deep on his blood-warm smell. I touched his ears and eyelids with my fingertips; examined the lilac almonds of his fingernails. What this baby would look like had not occurred to me. I certainly never expected him to be so perfectly beautiful.

'Will I take him?'

I nodded, there was nothing else to do; I had refused the offer to keep the baby with me for a few days, thinking it would be easier to break away immediately. The midwife stalled, as if she wanted to say something. My eyes pulled away from her face to Malachy's. My sweet baby. My son.

'Camera!' I said, relieved that I had remembered.

She placed Malachy on the bed beside me and pulled my camera from my bag. I took a few shots of him, blanketed and snug, his dark eyes roving, reading who knows what in the air about his face. I picked him up again and the midwife took a picture of me holding him; she took it quickly and I wanted her to take another in case it didn't turn out, but she was brusque now – killed with efficiency – so I didn't ask.

'All done?' she said, putting the camera back in my bag.

'There's a paperweight with my things. Take it; it's for him.'

She rummaged and held up the plumbago egg. 'This?'

I nodded. 'Oh, and there's a blanket and a hat.' I stared at Malachy while she fished them out of my bag.

'Is that everything?' the midwife said.

I nodded again. She pushed the paperweight into the hat, put it into the folds of the blue and green blanket then, tucking the bundle under one arm, she lifted Malachy from my arms and walked away. I sat and stared at the door through which they had left for a long, long time.

Chapter Two

Unlike the rest of the men who grew up in our area, Cormac is not now fat. He is hefty, stocky even, but he has kept his young man's shape. He is four years older than me – which seemed a lifetime when he was Dónal's big brother – but, of course, it is nothing now. His friends and our friends – old school pals and local kids – as well as all of our enemies, are suddenly adult and equal. We are in the same game: we birth late, struggle to pay off big mortgages, muddle through careers, and we watch our parents become the elderly of our neighbourhood.

Meeting Cormac again was like coming home. It wasn't just that he looked like Dónal, he was a grown-up, solid version of him. And he had a calm that roped me in; he drew me to him like the lunar pull on the sea. Cormac was newly returned from Australia when we met at a mutual friend's housewarming party. I had recently finished with my latest pointless boyfriend and we fell together and found it worked. Instantly, it worked. Within a year we were married and we did the whole bit: the Happy Ring House, the lace wedding dress and grey morning suits, bride and groom speeches, the honeymoon in Greece. A month after the wedding I was expecting our first child, whom we lost – our poor, half-born baby. Then I got pregnant with Nessa and she stuck.

Like the wall of a dam shouldering water, Cormac holds me up. He is absolute and fixed, a sure thing. I lie with him at night, soaking up his man smell: sweat and skin and spunk. I trace the zip of his spine and finger his sleeves of tattoos. I trail my hands across the inked feathers and the fish; the anchor; the roses and hearts; and the name

'Janelle' – his Australian love. He has offered to get a cover-up tattoo to obliterate Janelle, but I like the curl of the letters and the cutesie sound of her name. I used to razz him that if our baby was a girl we could call her Janelle but he didn't join in with the joke. He is too steadfast and serious for real teasing. With Cormac, I am beyond safe; he is the first man who has made me feel free from danger, cherished. At last I know that I have love. I no longer have to confuse desire, coupled with loneliness or grief, for love. This is it.

These days, within me, I hold a little of everything I understand about love and its loss: losing Dónal, loving Struan, losing my son, the grief over my miscarried baby, loving Nessa and Cormac. All of it swoops and collides inside, making me soar and crash, soar and crash. And Cormac and Nessa are, of course, the easy part of it all.

After Nessa was born and we were left alone in the delivery suite to get to know her, Cormac cried. I rubbed his shoulders as he sat on the bed, holding our daughter. I hadn't seen him cry since we got together. He couldn't speak and he tried to hold back the tears, but they emerged anyhow, on reluctant sobs and sighs.

'Do you want to talk?' I said, pulling a ragged, powdery tissue from my dressing-gown pocket for him; it was all I had.

'Ah,' was all he could say, another attempt to quell the crying. He dabbed at his face with the tissue.

'Is it your da?' I asked, knowing how new life and death get wrapped tight together, and his father was not long dead.

Cormac nodded, then shook his head. 'It's Dónal really.' He gasped and swallowed hard. 'It's that he never got to do any of this: meet someone, have a kid. Just to grow up. He never got the chance.' He kissed Nessa's head. 'Da and Dónal – they'll never meet her.'

I stroked his neck and kissed his arm; I lay back against the pillows and he put Nessa beside me. He told me he was OK, said he was sorry; he didn't want to upset me. The whole scene – Cormac with our daughter and his tears, the way he was fixed over her – made me love him more.

I dread Verity's visit to see the baby, sure she will arrive stinking of alcohol, her pores weeping the stuff all over me and Nessa. I am worried about what she might think, say and do. She avoided the maternity hospital, sending word that her 'ward phobia' meant she couldn't come and that she would see us at home.

But, like the dyed-in-the-wool contrarian that she is, Verity does not reek of drink when she arrives; in fact, she smells of Lux and her clothes are ironed. I am beached on the sofa, under the baby, as usual. She blusters in, her face alive, and I can tell it is not vodka that has her animated. There are no slack, soft edges to her eyes and her smile is real.

'Mother, you're flapping,' I say and, unlike herself, she giggles madly.

'Where is she? Where is this granddaughter of mine? Let me have her.' She stands over me, twiddles her fingers and reaches for Nessa.

I hand the baby to her. 'Say hello to your Granny Verity, Nessa. Granny, meet Nessa.'

'Oh,' she says, 'oh and oh and oh, would you look at her?'

Verity holds Nessa expertly, her long arm under her back; she sings her name into her face and smiles. Cormac lifts cushions, so that she can sit down on the sofa beside me. She doesn't say 'How will you cope?' or 'Imagine, you a mother!', which is what I have heard from some; Robin had a go, of course. Neither does she try to jolly me along, or pretend things won't be different or strange. She is – and here is a word I never thought I would use about my mother – perfect.

I lie awake, listening to the joyriders careen up the valley; boy racers in souped-up Hondas, tearing the arse out of the night. The rip and wheen of their cars is a familiar night-music; it makes me extra glad to be with Cormac and Nessa, the three of us snug in the one bed, cloaked in love. But I am sore and restless; day and night I want to lie in a hot bath to ease the pain, to make me feel OK. I want a magic shot of energy to take me through these few weeks.

My mind is alive with memories and questions – there is a constant drone in my brain – but I am so shockingly tired that none of it coheres. I stare at Nessa and try to remember what Malachy looked like. In my memory he is longer, bigger, a more solid prospect altogether; he had a rotund belly. Nessa is slender, girlish, slight. Even still, when I dress and undress her, I sometimes expect her to be a boy.

I slide from the bed and go down to the sitting room. By the light from a high white moon, I pick up and examine all the baby cards that are ranged on the mantelpiece. They have soothers on them and bunnies; teddies and ribbons; ducks and prams; they have acres of babies dressed in pink, pink, pink. I read the messages inside and let all the good wishes and congratulations seep into me like oil through muslin. I want to soak up the breadth and width of my good fortune and leave all else aside. My father and India sent the biggest card of all, one with a black Madonna and child, and it makes a curious contrast to the girly, swirly cards given by others. It looks out of place and it bothers me suddenly – its preachy serenity – so I shove it to the back, behind the rest of the cards.

I go to the window sill and stick my nose into the bunch of blush lilies that Cormac brought me in the hospital. I hear the ragged call of our neighbour's rooster, sending up his cries to the moon – does he never sleep? I breathe deep on the lilies and look up to watch the moon ride across the sky, a rolling pearl. This is me now, I think; this is who I am meant to be: mother to this child. All is well.

Chapter Three

I rang the doorbell but there was no answer. Struan had offered to make dinner for Robin and me that evening, but I thought I could corner him in the kitchen, or send Robin out for more wine, and tell Struan the news then. I was planking it. What was he going to say? What was *I* going to say? How the fuck did I even feel about it all?

There was no sign of either of them in the kitchen or sitting room, but I saw that their jackets were pegged in the hall, so I climbed the stairs. It was dull on the landing and I was about to turn on the light when I heard a low sound – moans and whispers. I stopped and listened; I could hear the wet slip of skin on skin. The noises were coming from the spare bedroom. I thought it might be Sam and her fella; I had never met him and I was curious to see him. But, no – they wouldn't be in there while Robin was staying with Struan, surely.

I walked slowly to the doorway and looked into the gloom: there were two figures in the room. My eyes adjusted to the dim light and I saw Robin. His hands were gripping someone's hips and he was moving against them. I tilted forward and saw the naked gleam of Struan's back; his head was thrown forward and his hands were fastened onto the saddle of the exercise bike. He was grunting and it was laced with a deep, animal pleasure. I gasped and Robin looked up; his eyes were glazed and his lips slack. He saw me, smiled, then turned his face away.

I had a slow, idiotic awakening as I watched the two of them. Coupling. Doing what lovers do. My camera was around my neck and, for some reason beyond knowing, I put the viewfinder to my eye and shot. *Flash, flash, flash.* By the fourth flash they were pulling apart.

I turned away and went into Struan's bedroom, walking like an automaton; I felt a caul slowly lift from my eyes. I stood by the shelf and picked up two paperweights, balancing them like a scales, one in each hand. I put them back and examined each and every weight on the shelf in turn. I peered into their teeming interiors: they held thistles, flowers, stars, droplets, milky swirls and colours of every kind. Their glass exteriors were smooth and cold. Such solid, magical things. They were sand once, I thought, lining them back up, though it was hard to believe. *Don't build your life on sand.* I held the millefiori paperweight, its centre a riot of mosaics that reminded me of old fashioned sweets. I loved its flowering hexagons that were stacked like the land-bridge that once linked Ireland's Causeway Coast and Staffa. I was fascinated by the way the glass magnified and shrank the flowers as I tilted the paperweight this way and that.

I picked up the plumbago egg – my favourite. I held my hands around it like a supplicant deep in prayer and pressed my nose and lips against it. Struan and Robin. Robin and Struan. I could hear them whispering fiercely in the next room; I could hear the rattle of belt buckles and the thump of feet emerging through trouser legs onto carpet. The fronds of seaweed inside the glass seemed to dance under my gaze; the rosy coral and the bubbles meandered and rose, like fizzing champagne. I popped the plumbago egg into my satchel, sat on Struan's bed, and waited.

I heard footsteps retreat down the stairs and the front door banged; the brass knocker thumped then settled. Struan came into his room and sat beside me on the bed. Neither of us spoke. He lit a cigarette and I listened to him draw the smoke sharply into his lungs in three short blasts. We sat, not moving. Someone shouted out on Clanranald Street; cars drove by; the ferry to the Isles let its long, lonely blast.

I turned to look at Struan. 'Well?'

'I don't want to finish this cigarette,' Struan said, mesmerised it seemed by the ash that would fall any second, 'because when I finish it, I think everything will have changed.'

'Everything changed long before that cigarette.' I stood up and went to the window. 'He's my brother, for fuck's sake.'

'There's nothing I can say.'

'You could try "I'm sorry", Struan. Or, "I'm queer". Or did that slip your mind somehow, ever since we met?'

'I am sorry. Of course I'm sorry.' He shouted the words at me.

'Don't raise your voice to me. I'm the one who should be ranting and raving.' I turned to face him. 'I feel like I've been reading a story where the beginning is missing. I feel like a fucking fool.' I dug the heels of my hands into my eyes and rubbed; I looked over at him. 'Are you gay?'

'No!' His denial fluttered between us, a bird searching for a place to rest. 'I'm sorry, Lillis. Really, I am. You have to believe me.' Struan came over to where I stood and put his hand on my sleeve.

'Don't touch me! He's all over you.' I pulled my arm away. 'Jesus Christ, I can't even look at you.'

I grabbed my satchel from the bed and, as I did, the paperweight I had taken rolled out and fell to the floor; it landed on the carpet with a thunk. We both stood, staring down at it. Struan bent, scooped it up and handed it to me. I put it back into my bag and left.

Every day I walked up the Byres Road, past the side street that held Pearl's pink house. The lights were usually on and I imagined her inside, in thrall to the television and the news it spat out to feed her. My heart would palpate in case Struan's car sat outside his mother's house; I never saw it there and that was both relief and disappointment to me.

I had a tiny bedsit in a Victorian redbrick off the Great Western Road. I worked lunchtimes in an equally tiny café called The Bonny Bird, mostly cutting sandwiches – endless square-sausage pieces with pickle, or thick cuts of ham dolloped with mustard. The bonny bird was an ugly silver parrot who could say 'Hello there' in different accents. His cage stood in the corner by the window and he climbed in and out, shitting on the floor underneath, screeking his hellos and burbling away to himself like a lunatic. He seemed to me like a health and safety inspector's dream but, for whatever reason, he – and the café – endured.

William, my boss, was an easy man. His wife Mary often sat in the café, her chair pushed back from the table, her palms curled over the high plum of her belly and a satisfied set to her face. She had the cushioned, ignorant look of the newly rich.

When my boss first introduced his wife to me I said, 'It's like an old ballad, where there's a William there's a Mary.' I laughed and William tittered politely, but Mary just looked at me, closing her hands on top of her bump as if she were the only pregnant woman in Scotland. I hadn't yet begun to show.

Over those months I spent most of my spare time lying on my bed. I read a lot and thought a lot, trying to figure things out. I went to the cinema often. I window-shopped around Sauchiehall Street. I knit a hat and blanket for the baby, clicking my needles feverishly into the night when I should have been sleeping. I was desperate to have the finished garments so I could look at them, hold them, fold and re-fold them. I made both in blue and green, for the baby's Scottish and Irish parts.

I was bloated with grief, though I wouldn't have named it that way then; grief to my mind was coupled with death, with memories of Dónal. This was a new kind of loss. My thoughts would slip back to Struan and Robin and I would try to sort it out in my head. Who had made the first move? Had they kissed? Did either of them even consider me? Who was to blame – Robin or Struan? They weren't drunk – it was early afternoon – had they smoked something? Taken something? It all left me confused and enraged, so I didn't let myself linger over it. I packed it away as something too sordid and hurtful to dwell on for long. And I found it hard to look forward, too; nothing seemed to fit in my life anymore, there was barely a place even for myself.

I would lie on my bed, reading the slim baby book I borrowed over and over from the library, marvelling at the author's pictures of herself, pregnant and giving birth. She was unafraid of her own nakedness in what seemed to me an untamed way. Her neat bump and long, wine-dark nipples offended me and made me impatient with her. If I had been asked, I couldn't have said why.

I wrote to Verity and told her things hadn't worked out with Struan and that I had moved to Glasgow to see how I might get on there. She didn't mention in her letters back if Robin had said anything about what had happened between him and Struan, and I didn't ask. She told me to be kind to myself. Robin didn't write.

I met the woman from the adoption agency several times and she encouraged me to choose prospective parents from her file, but I declined.

'You pick the best ones,' I said, and she gave me a look that I couldn't read.

She talked to me about having access to the adoptive family through photos and letters, but I said I didn't want anything like that. She asked if the father's name would go on the birth certificate and I hummed and hawed and eventually said it would. Then I said it wouldn't. Then I said it would.

At work, when it became obvious that I was pregnant, William installed a high stool behind the sandwich bar without comment and I cut the bread there every afternoon. He offered me early maternity leave, but I worked on and on until the baby's due date and past it. When I was a week overdue, I left The Bonny Bird for the final time.

On my last day, I had lunch in the café with William and Mary. Over William's shoulder, I watched the retreating behind of a young mother, wide and beautiful in linen trousers. She had a baby in her arms and a toddler at her shins; the toddler was pulling at her, making some demand. The mother slapped his hand but, instantly remorseful, she bent low and kissed his face. He sobbed a little, nodded and pouted his lips while his mother consoled him. I thought I heard Mary snap her fingers to get back my attention, but she mustn't have because, when I looked, her arms were still tucked across each other. It wouldn't have surprised me if she had.

'Will your chap be with you at the birth?' she said, rocking her baby's pram violently with one hand.

'Ah no. He's squeamish.'

'Just as well. Men are terrible at a birth; William was utterly useless, I had to tell him to leave. *He* was upsetting *me*.' She barked a laugh. 'What hospital?'

'The Queen Mother.'

'Oh, God, they're butchers in there. Butchers! My friend had to get a hundred stitches; her womb went septic. Why don't you travel to Edinburgh and go private? That's what we did.'

'Not everyone can afford what we can, Mary,' William said, quietly.

'Well, if it's a girl, let me know, Lillis. I have tons of clothes,' Mary said.

'I have all I need.' Seeing she was annoyed, I added, 'I will, thanks, I'll let you know.'

I watched her pluck the salad garnish from William's plate and eat it while he sat on, eyes ahead. There was a taut silence between us and I finished my sandwich quickly and got up to leave. William wrapped me in an awkward hug. He stuffed an envelope into my hand and told me to take care. I was grateful for the money; I was living, by then, on the clippings of tin, as Granny King used to say.

Looking back, I see a gossamer quality to those months – a suspension of life while life burgeoned inside me. I had removed myself from myself, as much as from the worlds I had occupied up until then: home and Kinlochbrack. Glasgow was a crevice I slid into and I stayed wedged in there until it was time to come out.

Chapter Four

Sometimes I feel the pull of my former self – the unwary girl who thought the bad, the odd and the difficult things happened only to other people. I fall backwards in my mind to the time before Dónal died, but it is hard to conjure the person I was then or what she was about. And it doesn't matter. My life is made up of all that has taken place and hard things happened before Dónal's death too.

Cormac and I have come to tidy Dónal's grave for his birthday; Treasa, their mother, would normally take care of it but she hasn't been herself since Mr Spain died. Desiccated snowdrops stand in the built-in vase beneath the headstone, and weeds hem the outside borders of the plot. It is a dry, bright morning and, though I am tired, the fresh air makes me feel lively. Sucking air greedily into my nose, I welcome the small surge of energy being outdoors brings. I kneel on a plastic square and pull knotgrass and shepherd's purse from the soil; their shallow roots make them come away easy. Cormac gently scrubs the gravestone with the soft bristle brush that his mother keeps for that purpose. I can hear teenagers shout and laugh on the crazy golf course across the fence.

Nessa sleeps in her pram beside us as we work; it is the same pram that both Dónal and Cormac were pushed around in as babies. I get up from my knees to check on her. She is bundled tight like an Eskimo – in coat, hat, mittens, baby-nest and quilt. I push up the hood of the pram.

'Leave it down,' Cormac says, 'she needs a little sun on her face.'

'She might get burnt.'

'There isn't much strength in an April sun.'

'Still.'

I leave the hood up and go back to weeding, but I am on high alert, thinking I hear the baby snuffle and stir. In the house, I have to have her in the same room as me always – downstairs in her pram, upstairs in the Moses basket. I came in from a quick trip to the supermarket one day and she wasn't where I had left her. My heart slipped up to my throat and lodged there; I thought I would choke.

'Where is she?' I shouted at Cormac, racing from room to room.

'Up in our bedroom.'

'On her *own*?'

'I have the monitor on,' he called after me as I ran up the stairs. She was fine, of course, but I simply cannot let her out of my sight.

Cormac soaks his brush in water and continues to clean Dónal's headstone; the shush of the bristles is soothing.

'The stonecutter is doing my da's inscription next week,' he says. 'There's not much space for it; Dónal is taking up too much room as usual.' He lets a short laugh. 'You know, we should buy a plot.'

I shiver. 'Don't say that. It's morbid.'

'It's reality, Lillis. The plots in the new extension are nearly sold out, I heard.'

'Where did you hear that?'

'My ma told me.'

I can hear fossicking noises from the pram. I get up and look in at Nessa; she is trying to get her fingers into her mouth. 'She's hungry.'

'Go on home and feed her, I'll finish up here.'

I take the bunch of bluebells I picked from our garden for Dónal out of the pram's under-tray and hand them to Cormac, then I push the squeaking pram through the hush of the graveyard. The wheels' controlled bouncing lulls Nessa back to sleep. The pathways are narrow and the place is deserted; I look at each grave that I pass – some are rich with statues of angels and photographs of the dead, others are nothing more than an iron cross with dates. One grave says, 'Here lies Loman Nulty, a gentle man', and I wonder if that was Mr Nulty who was our school caretaker. I speed past the graves holding children with their teddies and candles. Beyond the stone wall, motorists lightly tap their car horns, greeting their dead as they drive by. The sun drenches the yews that line the perimeter wall, making the trees seem less sinister for a while as they sway under the light. I count seven crazy golf balls dotted on the pathway like giant gobstoppers and wonder if the gravediggers toss them back over the wall before funerals are let in.

I push the pram up and over the long swirl of the flyover bridge that joins the two sides of the motorway, then walk along Beechlawn Avenue. Once inside the house, I settle into the sofa with the baby. The starfish of her hand against my breast is possessive and content, and her sucking is voracious. It pleases me that I am keeping her alive; me alone.

I am bone-weary and I fall into a half-sleep. My nights are disturbed not just by the baby but by my brain which click-clacks along like an overloaded train, rarely giving me a rest. I dream of babies who won't feed from me; babies who can talk; I dream that I am heavily pregnant but my stomach is malleable like bread dough. In this dream I am walking with the pram but when I bend over to fix Nessa's blanket she is not there; I let go of the handle in shock and the pram speeds away from me, of its own volition, and I cannot move. I dream that I am on Shore Street in Kinlochbrack, looking out on the loch; there is a child with me but I can't see his face. I know that he is Malachy. Something shifts and I dream that Cormac comes back from the graveyard and yanks Nessa from my arms – suddenly she is back with me! Cormac grabbing her makes the baby yelp and me scream.

Then Cormac is standing over me, returned for real. I fight my way to wakefulness and go to speak, but Malachy sits continuously on my tongue today and I have to bite him back before he falls out in front of Cormac. The 'M' of his name starts but I bury it in time and say, 'You're back.'

I shift Nessa's head; her mouth is thrown open like a yawning kitten's, wide and pink.

'Why don't you take her up to bed, get some sleep?'

'I won't be able to nod off tonight if I do that.'

'You're not sleeping anyway.'

'Maybe I could get some pills to help me?'

'I don't think you can take anything like that when you're breastfeeding.'

'No, probably not.'

'My poor tired dormouse.'

Dormouse was what he used to call me when I was able to sleep anywhere: in the car, on a bus, at the cinema. 'You could nap on a mantelpiece,' Cormac would say. Now I listen to the dawn chorus each morning and keep an almost satisfied account of the fact that I know the choir of birds starts up earlier every day.

Cormac leaves for work and I haul myself from bed and change the baby's nappy on the chest of drawers by the window. The pout between her legs is so tiny and perfect; I wipe her and think that I wouldn't know what to do with a baby boy. How do you wipe clean all that *they* have?

I have been obsessing about paedophiles – the radio news is full of them – and it frightens me to think of Nessa being abducted, like that little girl who was on holiday in Portugal and has never been found. I try hard to bundle these thoughts under better ones but they resurface, especially at night, and I weep into my pillow for fear of what could happen. I pull on Nessa's babygro and tell her she is the best girl.

'Aren't you my girl? My best girl? You are. You are. You're my only one.'

In the kitchen the fridge whirrs; its pitch gets higher and higher until it sounds like it will take off and burst through the ceiling and then the roof, like some mad rocket. The noise of it makes me want to scream and I leave my breakfast uneaten so that I can get away from it. I pull on boots, put a coat over my nightdress and bundle Nessa into her pram. The park is a couple of miles away but I crave to be there in the vast quietness and green. I push the pram past the terrace where my piano teacher lived; she probably still lives there – the house's name is unchanged on the fanlight, 'Saint Jude'. The patron saint of hopeless cases. I was hopeless at learning piano so that was a fit, I think. I pass the playground where a fat red-haired girl is slumped on a swing. I want to call out to her, 'Shouldn't you be at school?' but she looks so abject that I can't bring myself to speak. She swings desultorily and stares ahead. I pass the Used Cars for Cash garage with its tired bunting and defeated salesman, perched in the window like a dummy, staring out at the world.

The park's high wall makes a secret place of it. I go through the gate and feel calmer at the sight of all the grass that slopes away from me on both sides of the pathway. I hope a deer might come sniffing out from among the trees, like happened last time. It was a young deer with a red tag in one ear, separated from the herd – a maverick or loner. I watched for ages as it nosed about the ground, unconcerned by anything. No deer appears and I walk on.

There is a man sitting on my bench. I can usually time it so there is hardly anyone in the park but today there is a man on my bench. He looks forlorn, but I am irritated with him for taking my spot. I idle past, hoping he will move, but he sits on. I stop and lift my head to listen to the shush-hush of the horse chestnuts, newly in leaf. A pigeon leaps from a branch and bustles onto a lower one.

'Do you want to sit down?' a voice says. I look over at the man. 'I don't bite.'

He must know this is my bench; his invitation is a way to apologise to me. My chest swells. I wheel the pram over, put the brake on and sit. The floral end of my nightdress sticks out the bottom of my coat. All around the man's feet are pistachio shells, they are like fawn-coloured beetles, scurrying about. I look away, to the fresh leaves on the trees, their thick trunks.

'And how are you this fine morning?' the man says.

I stare at him. Why does he keep speaking to me? I ruffle the end of my nightie with my feet. 'I'm OK,' I say, stiffly.

'Isn't it grand to get a bit of fresh air?'

'It is.'

'The park is a great amenity. For the kids. For us all.' He smiles. 'Hah?'

'Yes, it's lovely.'

He toes the pistachio shells with his shoe. 'Isn't it great to be young? It's well for you.'

I smile tightly. 'Mmm,' I say. Is forty young, I wonder? It doesn't feel like it to me.

'Can I look in at your babby?' He is already rising from the bench.

'No, no, no.' I leap up, kick off the brake and grab the pram's handle. 'No. Keep away from her.' I shove the pram along the path, away from him.

'You fucking bitch,' he shouts after me. 'Bitch!'

I try to calm the histrionics that rise in my neck; I glance behind and he is on his feet, staring after me but he doesn't move to follow me. I push the pram quickly towards the gate and exit gratefully onto Chapelizod Road. I fumble for my handbag under the pram's apron but it is not there. I go to a phone box, thinking I can reverse the charges to Cormac at work and he will come and get us. But the receiver has been cut from the cord. The phone box stinks of piss, which makes me feel like throwing up, which in turn makes me light-headed. I stumble out, hang on to the pram and lurch forward.

I head for Verity's. Sometimes I rehearse things to talk about when I am on my way to her house, to get on her right side and ease my way into her mood, but not today. I can barely get up the road and my mind is loaded down enough without trying to prepare myself for my mother. Verity looks bothered when she answers the door, she hates anyone to call unexpectedly, but something about me makes her soften.

'Come in, come in,' she says, waving her hands and hurrying me into the hall as if she is afraid someone else might steal in through the door behind me. I bounce the pram over the threshold. 'What happened to you?'

'Nothing happened.' Tears drop onto my coat and I see them as if they are coming from someone else's eyes. 'Oh, Mam.'

She leaves the pram in the sitting room, helps me out of my coat and guides me up the stairs, where she puts me into her bed; I can smell her on the pillow.

'Try to sleep now.'

She leaves and I hear her slow clop on the stairs, then the ting that means she has lifted the receiver of the telephone in the hall. I listen to her murmur into the phone. I look at the wooden slats that make-up the ceiling; their deep honey colour is mesmerising and they lift a little of the darkness. None of the rooms are quite right in this house and they never have been. Curtains are sloppily hung; light fittings are crude and ancient, liable to electrocute you if you don't know each switch's knack. There is too much furniture: a dining table lives on the landing, saddled with five or six tablecloths and a pile of books; there is a wardrobe in the bathroom, skulking like an unwelcome guest behind the door.

My childhood home sits in the bowl of a valley; the slopes and the old, old sycamores and oaks cause long shadows, but there is another thing too – something created by Verity and Anthony, a dim oppression that hung over us always as a family. We weren't ordinary like our neighbours and, while I craved that as a child, I disdained it too. Verity and Anthony fought endlessly and with passion, then they would stay in bed for a day, making up, and Robin and I were allowed in to their room to witness how happy they were. *See*, their wrapped-together bodies beamed, *no more screaming! No more slapping! No more dish-smashing! All is well.* And, yes, it was a relief that the house was quiet, but things remained dark and we tiptoed around, trying to find ways to be good. Anthony took what little light there was with him when he left and we had to guide our mother from then on.

After a while Verity comes into the room again and snuggles Nessa into the bed beside me. The baby is still sleeping, her lips making sucking motions, then falling open to reveal the curl of her tongue, like a conch shell behind her gums. Nessa is the best thing that has ever happened to me, I think. I slip my finger into her fat little fist.

Verity sits on the bed. 'Babies are *real* work. They turn your life upside down and it's a high-wire act just getting through the day.'

'I'm tired, Mam. Exhausted, that's all. My head is fuddled.'

'That's to be expected. But is it anything more than that?'

'No.'

'Motherhood is immutable, Lillis. It's there and it's there and it's there. Nothing changes that. But you can get help.'

'Why are you saying that?'

'You seem distracted. Distraught even. Cormac says you're pacing the house at night. And you went out in your nightdress today, Lillis.'

'When were you talking to Cormac?'

'I rang him a while ago.'

'At work? Even I'm not allowed to ring him at work.' I throw off the quilt and she tells me to lie down. 'Rest, sweetheart. Feed Nessa now, then I'll take her and you get some sleep.'

'I don't want to sleep. I have things to get on with.'

'I'm telling you to rest and that's that.' Verity pulls the quilt up to my neck and mock strangles me with it. 'Feed your daughter then *go asleep!*'

She leaves again and I look at the framed embroidery of a peacock that sits over the mantelpiece. My Granny King had stitched the peacock – the most glamorous of birds – and managed to make it so disgustingly gloomy that it depresses me to even look at it. Verity barely mentions her mother and when she does it is with stiff words. Granny King – who died when I was very young – was, according to Verity, 'chilly'.

I picture my granny, an ancient version of me, of my mother, head bent low over embroidery silks, placing stitch after drab stitch into the sombre cloth, fashioning the peacock, like someone decorating a shroud.

When I told Verity I was pregnant with the baby I later miscarried, she was in a bad way. Her house was a shambles and she was acting maudlin and hopeless, letting herself and all around her fall into decay. Robin rang to ask me to try to sort it out.

'I can't face it anymore,' he said.

'Maybe she'll just drink herself to death; do us all a favour,' I said.

I knelt on her floor, a filthy cloth between my rubber-gloved fingers, scrubbing at unnameable stains. Verity was perched on the sofa, watching my attempts to right the mess.

'You missed a bit,' she said, and cackled.

'The drinking has to stop,' I said, 'for once and for all.'

'How dare you preach at me. What are you – perfect?' Verity leaned over and poked my shoulder with one finger. Her eyes were crackle-glazed.

'I never said I was perfect; this has nothing to do with me. You're killing yourself and you know it.' The bleach smell was making my stomach toss back on itself; I covered my mouth and nose with one hand. 'Things go wrong when you drink, you know that.'

'For your information, I haven't had a drink since Friday.' She pinched her mouth into an 'o', let her hands fall into her lap and stared at me. 'I woke up in a pool of piss on Friday morning, if you must know, and it shook me.' She looked at her hands. 'Even I saw that I'd gone backwards by about five years. That I'm regressing even as I age.' She smiled. 'The unfortunate thing is, sweetheart, my sorrows have learnt to swim – as someone once said – so drowning them isn't going to work anymore. Believe me, if I could knock their babbling heads under a vat of wine or vodka, I would.'

'Well, I'm glad you've come to that conclusion. You're a nicer person without drink.'

Verity sniffed. 'There's something hard inside you, Lillis Yourell. Something cold and hard.' As always she was resisting. Resisting the idea of a sober life; resisting the notion of herself as a decent person. 'I hate getting old,' she said. 'Such a gradual disillusioning; all the young desires end up looking silly and hopeless. It's sad but true.'

I got up from the floor and sat on the sofa beside her. My head was dizzy-heavy and I felt tired; I took off the rubber gloves and held my mother's hand. I wanted to do something to help her – my eternal desire. I thought I could cheer her up with my news.

'Mam, I want to tell you something.' I looked at her. 'I think I might be pregnant. In fact, I know I am.'

She smiled – a wicked curve of the lips – but her eyes remained fish-dead. 'Well, bully for you.' She snorted and snatched her hand away. 'You needn't think I'm going to mind it.'

She never apologised to me for her reaction to that pregnancy but, when I was expecting Nessa, she tried hard to be gentle and kind. And she tries still.

Chapter Five

In late November, Margaret came from Kinlochbrack to visit me in Glasgow. She sat in my bedsit, trying to look like she was impressed with the place, but she held herself away from everything. I was glad Charlie was not with her; I didn't want to deal with watching her change his nappy, feed and cosset him – I dreaded his very babyness. I made tea and we sat beside the window, looking down at the street.

'You could be a maternity model from a magazine, pet; that dress cleaving to your bump like clingfilm,' Margaret said.

I smoothed my dress over the egg of my belly, as if doing that might rub it away. The size of my stomach alarmed me most days.

'Have you seen Struan?' I said.

'Once or twice. He's cut up.'

'Well, he should have thought of that before, you know, having sex with my brother.'

'He's really sorry, Lillis. He seems depressed; very down. He's been neglecting the inn.'

I shrugged. 'Am I supposed to care?'

'Lillis, Sam came to see me.' Margaret put her hand on my arm.

'Sam?'

'Have you heard from her at all?' she asked.

'Me? How or why would I have contact with Sam? I can't stand her.'

'It seems she was in Glasgow a couple of weeks ago and she spotted you on Sauchiehall Street. Lillis, she knows you're pregnant.'

'Oh fuck. Has she told him?'

'That's what I don't know. She came to see me, to suss me out I suppose, but I didn't say a thing. I mean, I neither confirmed nor denied. I said she'd have to ask you.'

'Jesus, is there any way she'd say nothing to Struan? There isn't, is there? She's always been a horrible little shit. She'll love this.'

Margaret sips her tea. 'Lillis, you need to keep yourself stress free, for the baby. Don't dwell on it.' She shakes her head. 'But you know Sam. She's squibby – liable to go off at any moment.'

'You think she'll tell him?'

Margaret grimaced. 'Can *you* see her keeping her powder dry on this?'

I spent Christmas in Glasgow with Margaret, Gordon and Charlie. We stayed with Gordon's elderly father, who was confused about exactly who I was.

'Ah,' he said, a couple of times, 'you're Margaret's sister. I see.'

He was a congenial old man and I enjoyed the few days in his large house. We ate and chatted; dozed and played Scrabble. All the while I tried to ignore Charlie, who was too real, too present, too baby-like altogether. I observed the care that Margaret and Gordon took with him – everything was about Charlie – and curled myself away from it.

Two weeks after Malachy was born, I returned to Dublin. I watched the clouds below the aeroplane prancing like poodles, top to tail. Nothing would settle inside me and I was tired, so outrageously tired. A beautiful young man sat beside me on the plane, he was chiselled like a sports star from head to toe, and I had a mad urge to grab him and kiss his mouth. I didn't want to kiss him – not really – I just felt fit to explode; I was like a grenade with a wonky fuse.

Verity and Robin met me at the airport and I sat in the back of the car, taciturn and close-mouthed, all the way home. Neither of them spoke much either. I caught Verity looking at me in the rear-view, over and over, as if she had something she wanted to say to me, but couldn't get the words out.

145

Just like when Dónal died, I was pulled tight between forgetting and remembering. Any sense of myself as a competent human being, with things to do and achieve, had left me. I was a rag doll, floppy and useless. I signed on the dole and stayed in Verity's; I slept during the day, for hours and hours, and drifted through the weeks, doing little. I unscrewed the mirror from the dressing table in my old bedroom and put it against the wall, so I wouldn't have to face myself. Everything seemed pointless, even absurd. Why should I shower every day? Why should I eat proper food? Why should I care about getting a job, or socialising, or about anything at all? I woke up each morning without myself, glum with the realisation that I had to get through another day.

The after-blood seeped from me less and less and, as it waned, I wanted it back. Its smell was potent – meaty and ancient. That blood smell, for me, encapsulated the almost ten months I had carried Malachy. It took seven weeks and four days to dry up. Sometimes it felt like I had never given birth at all but, when I lay in the bath, my hands were drawn to the slack pouch of my stomach and the dark line that stretched up it. When the line and the pink stretch marks began to fade, I felt their loss.

Verity was always nearby; she would look at me for long moments as if wanting to scold me; sometimes she did.

'You're a malcontent, Lillis. Like me,' she said one afternoon, exasperated when I wouldn't get out of bed. 'Nothing pleases you. You wanted to come home. Now you're here but you won't do anything. Get up. Go out. You can't spend your life sleeping your brains to train oil.'

I did get up and I did go out. I met up with Robin's friend Fidelma for drinks. We sat in a city pub in dull silence. While avoiding me himself, Robin had somehow coaxed Fidelma into meeting me and, no more than myself, she clearly didn't want to be there. I asked how her café was doing and she told me it was going fine, but she didn't ask about Scotland or Struan or my future plans. I couldn't have talked about any of it anyway. I got drunk, sliding pints of lager into my throat like milk. The bar and its occupants became swimmy and I felt cantankerous and wrong.

'Why did you agree to meet, Fidelma?' I asked.

'Robin thinks we both need cheering up.'

I snorted. 'Robin knows fuck all about what I want. Why do you need cheering up?'

Fidelma agitated her hair with both hands and looked at the floor. 'I've been really low, totally all over the place.' She leaned forward and glanced around. 'I had an abortion a few weeks ago,' she whispered.

I couldn't even open my mouth to speak after she said it. I stood up from the table and left the pub, leaving Fidelma calling after me.

*

Malachy and Dónal are like twin ghosts; they swing together through my head and when one of them taps the wire of memory, it reverberates, then pulls taut and threatens to snap. I wake from dreams and think that I am still immersed in the dream-world, where everyone is together and growing older and all is well. The divide between my dream-life and my day is so ill-drawn that, one of these mornings, I am afraid I am going to blurt everything inside me to Cormac when I wake.

He has been urging me to join a mother and baby group, to meet other new mammies, but I am afraid I will be years older than all of them, so I wiggle out of it. I arrange to meet Robin for coffee just to get out of the house. I leave Nessa with Cormac. Though I fret about being away from the baby, I feel light as I take the bus into town, free for a while from her needs. I sit on the top deck of the bus and enjoy the swing up the quays, past the Luas, tinkling its way to Saggart, past the brewery and the barracks, past the bridges that bracelet the Liffey, each one named for a different man; past the green stretch of the river itself, named for a woman. My bus mates are either plugged into music or shouting into mobile phones; the graffiti on the ceiling is the same as it ever was: 'Macker 'n' Jean 4eva'; 'Ballyers are snots'; 'Jim Murphy is selling his wife Dolores'.

The boys on the bus occupy a seat each. The girls huddle together; they all have the same messy up-styles and heavy make-up along with matching tribal tattoos on their necks. I put my hand to my own nape, where the quaver sits, forever hidden under my hair. It is nice, I think, to sit on the bus, looking around, my mind emptying.

Town is quiet, most people are tucked up in their offices or busy after the school run. The quays reek of fried onions and the smell makes me momentarily hungry. I cross the Ha'penny Bridge and trot up to meet Robin outside a pub on Drury Street; he is already drinking coffee, sitting in the cordoned-off area on the footpath. He orders tea for me and asks how I am.

'I'm grand. Weary. But happy to be out and about.'

'You're bored out of your tree – I can tell.' He sucks on his cigarette, smirking. 'I'll never, ever understand why you married Cormac Spain. You're like peaches and *fake* cream. Polar fucking opposites.'

'I love him. He's a good man,' I say quietly.

'Don't make me puke. Since when have you liked *good* men? Jesus, you need a smack.' He swipes at the air with his cigarette and grins.

'Well, what I certainly didn't need was another quixotic arsehole like Struan Torrance.'

Struan's is not a name that is mentioned between Robin and me; he may as well never have existed as far as discussing him is concerned. What happened cleaved a gorge through us; we have never resumed the closeness we once had. Robin being Robin – and a true son of Verity – acted as if nothing had occurred. But it wasn't like that for me, it couldn't be. And so I pulled back from Robin and created a distance between us that he has not dared to breach. Or maybe by *his* actions he established the distance. Whatever the truth of it, we remain wary of each other. But, when we meet, we carry on in our own way, ignoring the past, and not looking down into the chasm. It is a case of whatever you say, say nothing, which has always been the Yourell solution to Yourell problems. He ignores Struan's name now, just as I knew he would. It doesn't suit Robin to talk about the past.

'Your downfall, Lillis, is you never know how to say no.'

'That's not true. Maybe when I was younger, but not now.'

Robin tosses his head, dismissing what I have said – a Verity move. He blows smoke at me which he knows I hate. 'So, what's your sex life like then, since baby? Is Cormac an animal?'

'Shut up. As if I'd tell you.' I bat the smoke away with one hand.

'I see; it's crap.'

I put down my cup and look at Robin. 'Why do gay men constantly bang on about sex? What's that all about?' He laughs. 'No seriously, tell me, I want to know. I mean, you all have jobs and homes, you go to films, to the pub; there's gay marriage to think about, politics, the recession, et cetera et cetera. Why is sex the *only* topic of conversation allowed?'

'Probably because we don't get any.' He takes my fingers in his. 'And just so you know, I don't give a fuck about marriage. It's not even vaguely relevant to me.' He flicks his ash onto the ground. 'I hate all that smug stuff that married people carry on with, like they're the only people on the planet. It's a look on their faces. You have it, even though you're miserable.'

'Oh, God, Robin, give it a rest. What is wrong with you today?'

'Nothing.'

This is how Robin operates when I am down: attack, attack, attack. He cannot stand when I am not lively, or going along with him in his banter. Like my father, he does not tolerate tears and bad humour. Anthony would leave the room if either Verity or myself cried when he lived with us. Or he would sit in grumpy silence until we calmed down.

We drink our drinks and sit without speaking. The forced gaiety of a group of girls near us bothers me. They are holding cigarettes between manicured fingers and they screech over each other, rather than talk; their eyes are insincere and troubled, and I find I cannot stop staring at them. One of them glances at me, then looks away. The whole group goes quiet and then they all laugh. They are clearly laughing at me.

'Fucking cows,' I say.

'Lillis, they're only kids.'

'Well, I can't be dealing with them. With anyone.' I drain my teacup and rise. 'Come on, let's go for a window-shop on Grafton Street.'

Robin sighs and finishes his coffee. He takes my arm and shuffles along beside me down Castle Market. 'Cheer up, Charlie,' he says, something Verity used to sing to us when we were little.

'I'm grand,' I say, and even I can hear the strain in my voice.

I get the bus back home; it stops on Wood Quay and the driver calls out the bus number. I look at the bus stop to see why he has done that and there is a blind woman standing there. She nods, smiles and rolls her eyes; it gives her a curiously calm look and, for a moment, I envy her. The doors sigh shut and we drive on.

I trail my hand along the bushes that are as snug as huts in front of every garden on Beechlawn Avenue. I put my key in the lock and, when the door opens, the quietness of the house assails me. I wander through the rooms and find them all empty. A small fur of panic coats the inside of my mouth but I tamp it down. Nessa is OK; she is with Cormac. Nothing can go wrong; he is not going to let her out of his sight.

I lie on the sofa and doze; I sleep for a while and wake suddenly with a clear memory of Margaret, staring at me across the tiny table where I ate my meals in my Glasgow bedsit, an angry set to her face. Margaret's eyebrows had a high arch which made her look constantly quizzical. It suited her because she was an inquisitive woman; not nosey, exactly, because that would imply a certain snoopiness. No, Margaret was just terribly interested in other people's lives and she shared the minutiae of her own in forensic detail. I knew everything about her family and far too much about her and Gordon's sex life, because she would muse aloud about it for hours at a time.

Margaret was disappointed with me because I was giving the baby up for adoption; it gnawed at her maternal self and she struggled not to mention it all the time. She also could not approve of the fact that I refused to tell Struan that I was pregnant but, at the same time, she seemed to understand that my hurt was huge and raw.

'In time,' she said, more than once, meaning that she was sure I would contact Struan eventually and tell him. But I never did. Months turned to years somehow and Struan slipped from the image I nurtured of the baby and me. He didn't seem part of it, that bubble of time where I carried and delivered our son. I thought – think – of Malachy daily but Struan rarely.

Margaret was particularly annoyed with me that day in my bedsit in Glasgow because she had asked if Struan could write to me and I said I did not want to hear from him. Ever. She didn't answer my refusal but she stared at me across my table as if I was the worst kind of brat she had ever encountered. In fairness, I probably was.

Chapter Six

A black sheep and her fat-haunched lamb sit on a rise ahead of me, serene as the Madonna and child. Fog skirls across the river and the daffodils on the bank lie almost flat from the dew. Dónal and I used to call that daffodil rain – the tiny drops that cling to the petals, bright as glass beads. I pluck one of the flowers and push my nose deep into its yellow bell, then toss it away. I examine my hands. I like that they are getting older – pallid and mottled and bony. They are a replica of Verity's hands; younger looking, but practically identical in shape and finger length and colour. I never knew that I wanted any part of me to be like any part of her, but I find I am pleased to see Verity's hands at the end of my arms.

My car idles by the gate, the exhaust jetting a steady stream. I walk to the middle of the field and throw my hands skyward, to see if I can feel the mist on my palms. I don't remember driving here.

Today is Malachy's birthday. My April boy. He is twenty, the same age Dónal was when he died. Twenty. It is a lifetime. A long time. Dónal was an April baby. My two April boys.

Yesterday there was another earthquake in Japan; the news showed elderly people, keening and hunched over, their faces a wreck of confusion and fear. I watched the footage for hours. Yesterday, too, I saw a dead crow hung above the garage of my neighbour's house, its torso a meaty patch. I could not figure out why it was there and I stood staring at it until Nessa woke in the pram. I rocked her back to sleep and continued to look at the bird.

I had seen a crow mobbing an eagle over the hills when out walking with Margaret in Kinlochbrack one day. She said the crow was protecting its nest, but I felt sorry for the eagle. I have always hated crows. The dead bird and the earthquake made me feel dark. Both of them are wrong things – things that should not happen, should not be seen or heard about.

Last night I had a déjà vu where Cormac took the place of Dónal in a long-ago conversation; it was like Dónal was in the room with me and I smiled at that thought.

'Why are you smiling?' Cormac said.

I was about to tell him but I swallowed it. I dread him knowing everything about me and I have a secondary dread that if he did know all, he wouldn't like me.

Cormac is madly content since Nessa was born; he occupies a space outside of me – the two of them do. I see them as a distant little unit and I look at them as if from a height. Even through his worry about me and my odd moods, I sense Cormac's deep satisfaction at being a father. Nothing I do or don't do dulls his pleasure at finding himself a daddy. And why should it? I am happy for him, jealous of him, proud of his pride in our daughter. She is perfect beyond reason, a baby like no other baby. Every grunt, every bodily evacuation – from her mouth, from her bum – is up for discussion. Cormac can talk about Nessa forever and ever, amen, and probably will. And I listen. But I am the pretend mother, not perfectly attuned in the way I should be if I could do this right. If only I could get it *right*.

Malachy is twenty. He arrived two weeks late; he was so well settled in my belly that it seemed he never wanted to come out. I wonder if he is unpunctual still. I wonder if he has my face, Struan's skin; if his hair is dark or fair. I wonder if he thinks of me every day, the way I think of him. Surely I will be on his mind today of all days.

The trilling of birds makes me look around; the hedgerow skirting this field is made of whitethorn bushes that look like they have been dipped in flour. I look down at the grass. My toes are looped around a dandelion stem; the field is dotted with their golden crowns.

I think of Margaret who was a friend to me; Margaret the good mother; Margaret who wanted to know everything about my life. She was always analysing the reasons why people are the way they are;

153

why they do the things they do. I learnt from her about the two sides we all possess: the public and the private, the show and the self. I let Margaret go too. I let everyone go in the end.

I know I cannot regain what is lost. Once I handed Malachy to the young Edinburgh midwife, I knew I would never get him back as he was at that moment. How could I? Even if I had returned to him after a week, to reclaim him for my own, he would have been different; a different baby to the baby I had left behind.

'My feet are freezing,' I say, and walk back to the gate and climb it. I stop to look at white lichen like splatters of liquid bird shit on the stone wall; I stand there examining the stones for ages. I get into my car and drive; the sun streaks through the window and warms my hair. I realise that I am three towns away from my hometown; I must have left the house at dawn.

I pass a church and the door is open. I check the rear-view and do a speedy reverse. Another car swerves and beeps; the driver is outraged. He bunches his fist at me and I look away. I park the car. This is not my kind of church: it is a square box, full of natural light. A woman walks back and forth across the altar, foostering with flowers and candles; she half-genuflects each time she walks past the tabernacle, a speedy nod to holiness, to what is right. I look for the Virgin statue and find her in an alcove. She is no more than a curved oblong of granite; her halo is part of her headdress and her feet stand on a stone moon. I am disappointed. What comfort can be had from this aloof lump of rock? How can I appeal to a featureless face? I pick up a handful of votives and throw them at the statue.

'You're a fake,' I shout, grabbing more candles from the stand and tossing them at the Virgin's head.

'Hey! Hey, you. Get out. You can't do that. Get out of here!' The woman from the altar barrels down the aisle towards me.

'Just fuck off,' I say, throwing the rest of the votives at her feet.

'I'm warning you. Out of here this instant, you pup.'

I sing along to the radio all the way home in the car; the DJ is playing songs I know – eighties songs – and I whack the steering wheel in time and laugh when I get the words right. When I turn into

Beechlawn Avenue, Cormac is standing in the doorway of our house, jiggling Nessa in his arms.

'Where were you?' he says.

'Nowhere.'

'Are you all right? I was worried, Lillis. And Nessa is hungry.'

I haul the baby from his arms. 'Learn to cope,' I shout. 'I won't always be here, you know.'

I plonk myself onto the sofa and let the baby feed. She guzzles and I feel my breast deflate as she nurses; the other breast, swollen and hard, leaks milk onto my nightie.

'You went out in your night things again,' Cormac says.

I look down at myself. My nightdress is stained; my feet are dirty and red with cold. 'I must have.' I pluck at the skirt of the nightie. 'It's like something you'd see in an asylum, isn't it?'

'Lillis, you're not coping. You need to go and talk to someone. Please?'

'I'll think about it.'

'Do, won't you? Ring the GP or something. Look, I'm sorry, but I have to go to work now. I'm two hours late already.' He bends down and kisses my cheek. He kisses Nessa. 'A package arrived to Verity's for you. She brought it over. It's there.'

I look at the package sitting on the dresser, a brown papered, boxy thing. So, they have been at it again; gathering together to discuss me. Shifty little meetings when I am out of the house. I lift Nessa to the other breast and close my eyes. I hear the front door shut and the whirr of Cormac's bike as he sets off.

My brain is like a colander; only one thing fits in it at a time and I have to strain that away before something else can take its place. But, no, that's not really it at all. My head is too full of things – Malachy, Nessa, motherhood, time, Cormac, housework, my *real* work and getting back to it – but I am not able to concentrate on any one thing. So it all soups together until I am breathless with confusion; mired in some muddy place that makes no sense to me. My mind cannot seem to get a grip on anything relevant and the minutes, hours, even the days steal past so that I don't notice them going. I am topsy-turvy.

155

When Malachy was born I lost one self, but there was no new self to replace the old me. I wasn't a mother to anyone – my family didn't know I had given birth; no one around me knew. So I shed one Lillis but couldn't fit inside the new one, because Lillis the Mother didn't exist. Now she does exist – I am a mother in front of the world – but I feel like a fraud. I am supposed to be delighted and serene, but I feel at odds with myself and irritable. There is no quiet time, no thinking time. There is just baby time.

I have been trying to unravel the facts of my life in Scotland all those years ago, but maybe that is a mistake. Maybe I should leave it wefted in the unweaveable mass it has formed inside me.

Nessa cries – she doesn't cry often – but I can't put up with it. I beg her to stop; I shout at her; I agitate the pram. She wails. Then I feel guilty; she doesn't know she is upsetting me. I look at her indignant red face; she is asking for something and I have little to give. Sometimes I do not want to feed her. Sometimes I don't even want to be near her; I want peace and silence; a place to be by myself.

'Please stop crying. Shush, Nessa, shush. Baba, be quiet. Come on, my head hurts. I'm tired. Shush. Come on, shush.' I bang the hood of the pram with my palm. 'Oh, for fuck's sake, just shut up.'

Nessa stops and sucks a deep breath, her face is a lavender rumple and she lets an almighty shriek. Now I have frightened her; I've scared an eight-week-old baby and I feel like the worst mother in history. I lift her rigid, screeching body from the pram, put her over my shoulder and walk the sitting room, up and down, until she is calm enough to feed. I sit on the sofa and watch her eyes roll as she suckles; I feel the distress hiccups bouncing through her tiny frame. She settles and, with her, I settle a bit too.

It occurs to me that I might be like Verity – exasperation was her fallback position, her natural state as a parent. Everything Robin and I did irritated her. She roared at us from one end of the day to the other: *Get out of my sight. Go out and play. Get off me. Leave me alone. Fuck off out of here and leave me be!* She struck us for the smallest of misdeeds, with her fist, with the wooden spoon, with whatever paintbrush or scalpel she had in her hand. Verity held the neglect she learned as a daughter to her heart and carried it forward to her own parenting.

I do not want to be the mother that Verity was to me.

*

When I was seven months pregnant with Malachy, Margaret invited me north for a few days. Not to Kinlochbrack but to Thurso. I took the train, changed at Perth, and met Margaret, Gordon and Charlie at Inverness. They stood on the station platform, their faces wide with welcome.

Curdled clouds hung above us as we drove north; Gordon leaned over the steering wheel to get a better view of the sky and cursed. Margaret gave out to him for using bad language in front of Charlie and me. Then she strained her own face upwards.

'It's not looking promising, right enough,' she said.

On the road outside Brora an empty hearse bowled past us, its driver dressed in green tweed. We stopped at both Golspie and Helmsdale so I could pee, which I apologised for over and over; I was forgiven with equal effusion. It felt like the baby was using my bladder as a pillow. I was utterly exhausted by the journey – it took a whole day to get to Thurso from Glasgow – but I was delighted to be away from the city and The Bonny Bird. Margaret and Gordon were in great form and Charlie slept in his baby seat beside me in the back of the car.

I watched a swoop of starlings flitter and dip like one huge bird as we drove; hundreds of black arrowheads, plunging and flocking before their nightly roost. We passed croft after empty croft, snugged under withered thatch, and the odd tourist coach full of grey heads, heading south.

We stayed in The Pentland Lodge and Margaret came to my room to tell me they had a surprise for me. My heart dropped to my boots in case this surprise involved Struan, but I knew by her manic grin that she had something cheerful planned.

'What is it?' I asked. 'Tell me, Margaret!'

She laughed and clasped her hands. 'We're going to see the Northern Lights.'

'Really? I don't believe it.' Struan had talked more than once about showing me the lights.

'We'll let you get your rest tonight, pet, and tomorrow night we'll go and see what we can see.'

We spent the next day lolling around the lodge. I was quite happy to sit with my feet up on the sofa in Margaret and Gordon's room, drinking tea, and watching Charlie arrange his farm animals on the blue tartan carpet. He was shy with me to start but soon he would gander past me with his eyes turned up, making sure I watched his prancing and play. He held animals aloft for me to name and I grabbed at them, saying 'Mine!' to make him laugh. We hooted animal noises together and I sang 'Old MacDonald Had a Farm' again and again. He never tired of doing the same things and his parents indulged him in that always.

Margaret called Charlie 'The Baby' but to me he was now a child, or a toddler at least. The only baby in the picture, as far as I was concerned, was the one making a broad paunch of my middle. Gordon had endless nicknames for Charlie – The Charlster; Chappy Chops; Muck Boy; and, weirdly, Wee Egg – so that half the time I didn't know who he was talking about. They were unassailable, Margaret, Gordon and Charlie, but I don't think I felt jealous; I had discounted myself as a parent and so what they were – their tight little trio – didn't seem to tally with what I was doing at all.

Gordon lay on their bed and read from the tourist brochure: ' "The Northern Lights are known in Scots Gaelic as *'fir chlis'*, which means 'nimble men' or 'merry dancers'." How about that?'

'That's you and Charlie. You are the *fir chlis*,' I said.

Gordon jumped off the bed and took Charlie's hands in his; he danced him around the room. 'Look, we're the Northern Lights! Look, Mummy, look! Can you see us, Lillis?'

Charlie threw his head back and pushed out a forced, throaty laugh – one of his new tricks. Margaret shook her head and smiled, quietly thrilled with the antics of her husband and son. She got up and the three of them jigged around the room before flopping onto the carpet to set up Charlie's farm properly. I started to nod off – their voices became as thick as velvet around my ears – so I went to my own room to lie down. As soon as my head hit the pillow, the baby started to writhe inside me. I rubbed at my stomach to try to calm the poking limbs, but the jostle and whirl went on and on.

It was near midnight when we left the lodge and joined the other people who were hoping for a view of the aurora. We were upbeat – the clouds had lifted. Our guide marched us down to the seashore; I waddled behind the group and Margaret slowed to keep me company.

She stopped and grabbed my arm. 'Jesus,' she said.

'Oh, my God.'

We stared ahead; Scrabster lighthouse flashed in the distance. Strung between it and Dunnet Head was a sweep of lime-jelly sky. Golden beams shot vertically up through the green and the whole band of light shimmied and swayed.

We stood and gawped and Margaret's hand shook where she gripped me. Gordon came back to us, pushing Charlie's buggy at speed, and there were tears dripping from his eyes.

'Have you ever seen anything like it?' he said, and let such a wild laugh that Charlie leapt in his sleep. 'Will I wake him, Margaret, to show him? Come on, let's get him up.'

'Better not.' She wiped the tears from Gordon's cheeks and kissed him.

Gordon moved to stand on my right and Margaret was on my left and they both linked me. We stared up at the bouncing lights; the sky above them was navy and specked with the silver of more stars than I had ever seen in one night. Our guide talked about the solar wind and excited photons but we just stood there, Gordon crying, and Margaret and me letting squeaks of excitement. Margaret handed Gordon a tissue and she whispered to me that it had been his life's ambition to see the aurora borealis. We stayed there for ages, gazing upwards, our eyes roving greedily over the colours, the flitting movements, the absolute magic of it. I lifted my camera and took a whole roll of film of the lit-up sky.

I soon got tired of standing; I had that late-pregnancy ache between my legs – the one that feels like the baby might topple out any second because of the fierce downward pressure. I said I would return to the lodge but they wouldn't let me go alone, so we trooped back together. As we walked Margaret put her hand on my bump. I saw her glance at Gordon and he nodded.

'Lillis, we need to talk to you about your baby.'

'Oh, yeah, what about it?' I wanted her to take her hand from my stomach; I didn't like the acquisitive way she let it lie there.

'If you're determined to go through with the adoption, why give the baby to strangers?'

'What do you mean?' I could guess exactly what she meant, but I needed to stall her from going any further; I didn't want to hear what she was about to say.

'Gordon and I have been talking and we feel we could give the baby a good home. A good life.'

Something white-hot ran through me and pinched at my brain; my head seemed to disconnect from my body. 'No. That's not possible,' I said, lifting her hand from my belly.

'Maybe you could think about it, hen,' Gordon said, his eyes puffy from crying. 'Think about it tonight and we'll talk in the morning. Or soon.' Like Margaret, he had a way of looking at you that always seemed reproachful.

'I made my decision months ago, Gordon. I've signed forms and everything.'

'But nothing is set in stone until you sign the final papers,' Margaret said. 'We would welcome your little one as surely as we welcomed Charlie into our lives.'

I wanted to bite her; I wanted to prick their cosy superiority with a viciously appropriate barb. But nothing would come.

'My baby won't be brought up in Kinlochbrack,' I said finally, forcing the words through my teeth. 'How can you even ask me this?'

I kept pace with them back to the lodge, though I wanted to storm ahead. I couldn't look at them and my face ached. I felt drained and deflated, and I needed to climb into my bed and block them, and their request, out. But when I got into bed I couldn't sleep; I lay awake for hours, feeling angrier and angrier with Margaret and Gordon. How dare they mess with my life? How dare they presume to know what was best for my baby or for me? After what Struan had done, how could they even think of raising my child with him living only a street away?

The next day, they dropped me to Inverness in their car. I stared dully at the passing scenery as we drove south; another fly-by of starlings moved in a huge chatter across the sky, but I couldn't muster much interest in their plummet and flurry. Our goodbyes were subdued on the train-station platform. I didn't see Margaret again until after Malachy was born and she never again mentioned the subject of taking my baby for her own.

The last month that I was pregnant with Malachy, I spent hours tracking his movements under my skin; the triangular hump of an elbow or knee would travel liquidly – a shark fin through water – and I watched it like a spectator sport.

'Would you look at that?' I'd say, to no one at all.

In the ninth month, I would lie on my side on my bed and it sometimes felt like the baby was scratching the inside of my bump, trying to claw its way to the light by any means. *Let me out, let me out.*

'Stop that,' I said. Or, 'Ouch, that hurt!' but the scraping continued.

Sometimes the movements got so wild that I would have to stop whatever I was doing and hold onto something solid; I winced and waited for the kicking to pass. I christened that jiggery-pokery. I sang 'Jiggery-pokery, jiggery-pokery' to my bump to the tune of 'Drops of Brandy', hoping it would make it stop.

At the cinema, if the film I was watching became explosive or loud, the baby jumped about in time, making me feel giddy and restless. I often left before the end of the film, the baby's kicks driving me to crave forward motion for myself. I would walk and walk – slowly and deliberately putting in the miles – knowing that it could bring on labour. I was impatient to be out the other side of the pregnancy; to be free of the wriggling, moving mass under my skin.

Nessa never kicked ferociously like Malachy did; she lay low inside me like a resting trout and sometimes I worried that she was not really there. I used to tap on my belly to wake her up. And Cormac sang to her, kneeling on the floor in front of me, his hands cupped around my gym-ball stomach as if he might suddenly jump on it and roll away. Unlike Malachy, Nessa did her forty weeks of growing with a stealthy ease.

I took photographs of my bump which, at the end, seemed to start at each hip and spread hugely, both out and around. It needed to be big to contain all of Malachy, who was a hefty baby. Later, I stashed those photos in a brown envelope in my knicker drawer in my mother's house, with the pictures of Malachy and the one the midwife took of me holding him. I thought that Verity had gone through them once – they seemed mixed up – but I couldn't be sure.

My skin looks grainy in the pictures and the triangle of moles that used to cluster around my belly button is spread out, gone awry. If you didn't know what you were looking at you might not guess that it was an expectant mother's stomach, raw with stretch marks. I wasn't half as interested in my changing body on Nessa; I was so terrified of losing her that I created a distance between me and the pregnancy. But I was busier too – with work, with loving Cormac, with watching out for my mother and her mayhem. When Verity became especially twitchy and blunt, I knew a fresh disaster was about to unfold, and some of it was to do with my impending motherhood, I was sure. I began to believe that she was jealous. She would talk about how easy women had it, not like in her day. And she would give me parenting advice which usually went along the lines of her hoping I had a boy because girls were 'little bitches'.

'Not everyone feels the way you do about being a mother,' I said to her once.

'People don't admit it,' she said.

'Admit what?'

'I don't know...ambivalence.'

'Plenty of parents adore their kids.'

'And you think you'll be one of them?' She snorted and laughed into my face. It was that laugh that offended me the most.

Chapter Seven

My GP recommends that I go away.

'Can you afford a holiday?' she asks.

'Yes. But even the idea of it makes me feel tired. All that airport nonsense.'

She smiles. 'A change is as good as a rest, as they say.'

'I might go somewhere. I'll speak to Cormac, see what he thinks.'

I look up at the Spire, probing at the clouds like a giant silver finger. All it needs is a thimble, I think, slowing to toss back my head for a better view.

Verity shades her eyes and looks skywards too. 'So bloody beautiful. There's hope for man yet, Lillis, when he can produce something as gobsmacking as that.'

She is molly-coddling me, on Cormac's instruction. We have come into town to shop but we don't know what to do with each other and there is nothing I want to buy. We are standing at the top of Henry Street like two lost children. We turn and walk up O'Connell Street, looking for a coffee shop. By the time we have passed Dr Quirkey's Good Time Emporium – surely, I think, the most disheartening place in Dublin – I realise we have gone too far. I take Verity's arm and we cross the street to the Kylemore Café. A homeless man sits on the traffic island, his face ripe with improbable bulges, his head nodding into sleep or, maybe, sobering awake. He is wearing a green cap with the slogan, 'Today I am Irish, tomorrow I'll be hungover!' It makes me want to weep. By the time we sit down with our coffee and cakes, I am seething with some unfathomable anger and I long to be alone.

We carry on in silence, slicing éclairs into bite-sized lumps and stirring sugar into our lattés. I watch two schoolgirls in green and scarlet uniforms grimace at each other through their braces, while they poke at lettuce leaves and slivers of chicken.

I turn to Verity. 'It pains us to spend time together like this, so why do we bother?'

'Lillis, I'm making an effort for you. I'm here, amn't I?'

'I don't particularly want you to be here. *I* don't want to be here; I'd rather be at home, asleep.'

'You can't spend your life in bed.' She licks cream from her finger and leans forward. 'We are alike, you know, me and you.'

'Alike and unalike.' I grunt. 'And I know for a fact that you don't relish the *you* that you see in *me*.' I toss my napkin over the remains of my cake. 'The GP says I should go away for a few days. She thinks I have a touch of PND.'

'In my day, we just got on with it.'

'See, this is exactly why I don't want to be around you.'

'Well, maybe you should go away; it might be good. Would you go on your own?'

It bugs me when she turns like this, suddenly reasonable and calm as a cow.

'Yes.'

She looks doubtful. 'Cormac and myself could manage Nessa between us, I suppose. Treasa Spain might take her for a few hours, if she can drag herself out of her pit long enough.'

There is no point in reminding Verity that Treasa is grieving for her husband; she has no sympathy for anyone, even though she is a wallower herself, over the smallest thing.

'The newspaper is doing a feature on the Scottish Highlands. I've got the gig for the photos.'

'You're going back to work already?' Verity leans across the table and starts to pick hairs from my jacket, but I push her hand away. 'When I was newly married women didn't run away from their children the way they do now.'

'It's one small job. I'll see how it goes.'

164

'Scotland. It might be nice to go back.' She eyeballs me. 'Will it?'

'Maybe.'

The package is heavy. Inside the brown paper there is a white box. I snip the tape holding the lid down with my nail scissors and take out the bubble-wrapped object inside. As I undo the plastic wrapping, I realise what it is and my gut liquefies. I stumble backwards and sit on the bed; I lift it out of the bubble-wrap, then hold it up to look at it through the light from the window. It is the plumbago egg. My insides start to fizz and pop and I barely make the bathroom where diarrhoea jets from me like water. I hold the paperweight and sit on the toilet, hugging it to my chest. I lift it to my lips and kiss the cold glass.

Cormac picks up the plumbago egg from my dressing table.

'That's gorgeous. Where did it come from?' He holds it to his face and wraps his two hands around it. 'God, it's lovely – it looks like there's a jelly fish swimming in it.'

'It was in the package that arrived the other day.'

'Oh? Who sent it?'

'I don't know.'

Cormac puts down the paperweight. 'What do you mean you don't know?' He sits on the end of the bed.

'Well, I do know. Someone from Scotland sent it.'

'Is it to do with the article for the newspaper?'

'Yeah. That's it.'

The television hums. I am watching the royal wedding from my bed; Cormac has provided tea, toast and orange juice, and Nessa sleeps obligingly between our two pillows. The camera settles on the queen; throughout the ceremony she can barely muster a smile, certainly not a genuine one. For once I identify with the woman; for once I feel I am much like her: a bag of misery.

'I wish I was going with you,' Cormac says, easing himself onto the bed so as not to wake the baby. 'I'd love to see the Highlands.'

'It's work; I won't have time to do anything fun.'

'I suppose.'

'Next time, OK?'

Cormac lifts my fingers to his lips and kisses them. 'It reminds me of our wedding,' he says, indicating the TV. We sit hand in hand watching the gorgeous young bride, looking outrageously relaxed, as she steps into her new life.

Nessa is offended by the bottle. She wraps her tongue and lips around the silicone teat and tries to suck it into shape but it doesn't work; she wails in frustration. Cormac rocks her and I perch opposite him, at the kitchen table, watching.

'Maybe I should put her to the breast.'

'Give her a chance; she'll get there.' He croons into Nessa's face and rubs her cheek with his pinkie. He drips some of the milk into her sobbing mouth and she falters, stops. He eases the bottle between her lips again and she suckles, grunting and stop-starting to let us know she is not pleased, but she feeds on. 'Now,' Cormac says, smiling at me. 'Off you go.'

I have been expressing for weeks, building up a store of milk for my few days away, and today I am going back to the office for the first time. Only for a couple of hours, to discuss the Scotland piece with the editor of the travel section; to see what she wants. I, naturally, have some ideas of my own.

The fridge shivers as if it is trying to shake off something. I flutter a bit, wondering if I should stay at home with Nessa. I am so used to being manacled to the house and the baby that I don't like leaving. I don't want to leave.

'You'll be OK?' I ask.

'We're grand. Look at her – she's guzzling.'

'Well, if you're sure.' I watch Nessa's eyes rolling back in her head like they do when she is feeding from my breast and I can't help feeling a little betrayed. I slip my arms into my jacket and kiss them both: Cormac on the head, Nessa on her cheek. 'See you later,' I say, and pull the front door gently behind me.

At my desk, I take the slip of paper that came with the paperweight from my purse. It is a small piece torn from something bigger; the blue-inked digits are clearly a phone number. I google it but nothing comes up. I google the area code and get back a list of musical names: Auchterarder, Blackford, Comrie, Crieff, Dunning, Madderty, Muthill, St Fillans.

I say them aloud, tasting each one in turn, '*Auchterarder. Blackford. Comrie. Crieff. Dunning. Madderty. Muthill. St Fillans.*'

To my ears, Madderty and Muthill sound made up. I type the names into the search engine one at a time and read about each town. All of them are in Perthshire. Auchterarder is the 'Lang Toon' because of its mile-and-a-half-long high street; its website is bordered with thistleheads, making it look quaint, like a site that was fashioned before websites existed. Comrie, I find out, lies directly on the Highland Line. St Fillans is a tiny village on a loch. I pour over the images of Dunning, where a saint once killed a dragon, and imagine Malachy learning all about the legend as a boy at school. There is a bowling green there and low mountains fence in the village; a lot of the photographs are of huge snowfall on streets, on cars, on mountains.

So Malachy lives in Perthshire. Somewhere in Perthshire. I toy with the telephone number, then put it back into my purse.

Chapter Eight

I take out the envelope containing the pictures of Malachy. I flick through the photographs of my bump to get to the one where I am holding him. It is not a great picture, the angle is skewed and the midwife didn't zoom in, so we are far away on the bed. Malachy is a little yellow bundle, tilted towards the camera. I look at the ones I took of him myself: his face is a bunched up red, bruised from the forceps and pickled from being so long inside me. His hair is black and plastered to his head in little streaks; I can remember the smell of him.

I look at the one of us together again: I am in a navy striped nightie and underneath the blanket, out of sight, it is patched with blossoms of blood. My hand is a mess of wires where an antibiotic drips into me to bring down a high temperature. I am so young in the photograph, a bit fat-faced, and my eyes are wary and exhausted.

Even though I think of him every day, at some point I stopped believing the story that these photographs tell: that I gave birth to a baby boy once. That I have a real, live, grown-up son. I slip the pictures back into the envelope and put it into the bottom of my jewellery box. I stand over Nessa in her Moses basket; she is awake, twisting her head and sucking her fingers.

'Hello, baba,' I say, 'hello, my gorgeous girl.'

Nessa smiles, a shy quirk of her mouth that ends in a gaping, gummy grin. She coos. I lift her out of the basket, which she is getting too big for now, and lie onto my bed and put her to my breast. The very smell of her is addictive: the heat of new skin and slightly unclean hair.

Margaret came to see me one last time in Glasgow. I was back in my bedsit off the Great Western Road, resting after the birth, and feeling curiously calm. I put on clothes for her visit, shedding the nightdress that was like a comfort blanket, the one I had given birth in. I put on blusher and lipstick to brighten me up. I didn't want her to think that I had been defeated. The air in the bedsit was stale, I knew. It was an autumnal April, blowy and cold and wet. I kept the window closed because I needed to trap all the heat that I could in the cocoon of my room. I knew the place smelt of mildew because I caught a whiff of it every time I opened the door after being outside. But it also held other smells: the chips I had eaten the night before; the human smell of my sheets and, possibly, the tang of the blood that still seeped from me. I had sprayed deodorant around before she came, but it wouldn't have made much of a difference, I was sure.

Margaret brought me Gordon and Charlie's love, and a bag of presents: dream rings from the bakery on Shore Street in Kinlochbrack; a statue of an angel made of soapstone; bubble bath; a bunch of white tulips; and a card with 'It's a boy!' written on it.

'I wasn't sure about the card but, one way or another, you're a mum now.'

'Thank you, Margaret.'

I stuck the tulips into a pint glass from the kitchenette and placed them on the mantelpiece above the boarded-up fireplace. Margaret told me news from Kinlochbrack. Sam had left the Strathcorry Inn suddenly and no one knew where she had gone, but there were rumours about stolen money and a bruising row with Struan. One of the fish farms in the bay had been sabotaged and all the salmon smolts were lost. Gordon had organised a pub quiz in The Windhorse and Struan's team won.

She glanced at me when she mentioned Struan, but I didn't ask anything about him.

'What weight was the baby?'

'Ten pounds, four and a half ounces.'

'My goodness! A bonny lad.' She combed her fingers through the fringe of her scarf. 'And the birth?'

'Forceps.'

'Ouch. You poor pet. Did you name him?'

'I called him Malachy. Malachy Dónal.'

'And how are you doing?'

I yawned. 'I'm OK.'

Margaret stayed for another hour or so and, when she was leaving, she hugged me tight, then held me away from her. 'Stay in touch, Lillis. Promise?'

I nodded and when I heard the front door close behind her, I went to my window and watched her walk down the road away from me, knowing I would probably never see her again.

Glasgow sang me to sleep during my last two weeks there: the police sirens and endless traffic became my lullaby. Though I was hollow and listless, somehow I slept not just at night but during the day too. These were heavy sleeps, ripe with dreams that I couldn't pin down when I woke; dreams that dragged off me through each morning though they were formless. By the time I left I was ready to go home; I couldn't wait to put the Irish Sea between me and Malachy, so that it would all be properly done, with no possibility of going back.

After feeding Nessa, I stand at my open bedroom window and watch a swallow loop and belly-flop, glide and flip above the toilet-brush trees that edge the green opposite our house. The swallow flies excitedly, as if taking part in a game. Soon another swallow starts the same ritual and the two birds sail past each other, up, around and over, before stopping on a telephone wire, their tails twitching. Then they are off again, too restless to sit for long. The evening is hot but still there is the smell of turf smoke; some people cannot give up the comfort of the fireplace, even in high summer.

Cormac comes home from work and, after dinner, I watch him read his paper on the sofa – this is when I desire him most, when he is a small bit out of reach. He folds the newspaper, lifts Nessa onto his lap and gazes at her. She stares back at him, her face serious.

'How was she today? Were you good for Mammy?'

'Babies can only be good; it's all they know.'

'I mean did she cry much?'

'She was an angel.'

'Good girl, Nessa. Are you Daddy's girl? Are you? Are you my angel?'

Cormac has a *ragù* lipstick from dinner; I point to my own mouth and rub. He looks at me quizzically, so I take one of Nessa's wipes and clean around his lips.

'Now, all nice and fresh.' I kiss him, long and deep, and he pulls me onto the sofa beside him.

'I love you, Mrs Spain.'

'And I love you, Cormac.'

We sit, the three of us, late into the evening, letting the room grow dark around us, listening to one neighbour's lawnmower, and smelling the charred meat of the other neighbour's barbeque. Nessa falls asleep in Cormac's arms so we go up to our room and place her in the Moses basket. Then, for the first time in months, we undress each other and make love. His body is like home to me, an extension of myself. Cormac falls asleep first and I lie against his chest, listening to the babumph of his heart, feeling the sweat dry into our skin.

Chapter Nine

We go to Galway for my birthday, shooting down the motorway's treacle-smooth surface, passing the Eddie Stobart trucks and the camper vans with identikit couples perched up the front, staring ahead. It is a grey midsummer's day, wet and drab, but I am in high spirits, for the first time in ages, it feels.

'I'm having wine tonight, nothing can stop me,' I say, and Cormac glances at me in the rear-view and smiles.

'You can have champagne if you want.'

'I'll pump and dump. Nessa can have some of the milk from the cooler bag. Can't you, Ness? Hey?'

I lean forward to talk to her; she is strapped into her baby seat in the front, content as a miniature Buddha. She lifts her head to peer around the side of the chair at Cormac.

'Hello, Missus,' he says, 'hello, Pooch.'

Nessa smiles and flops her head back; she grabs at her feet and makes coodling noises. The fields on either side of the road are filthy with buttercups, and shorn lambs shadow their mothers across the grass. I watch calves gambolling around the legs of static cattle, as if they are playing a game of chasing. A brown calf stops to suckle a black cow and his friend runs on, kicking his heels. Young animals, in all their happy vulnerability, always remind me of babies. The further west we go, the more burgundy bogland straddles the motorway; the bogs stretch to the horizon and are rimmed now and then with conifers. I see the word 'LOVE' painted in huge red letters on the strut of a bridge and, as we pass, I silently applaud the optimism of the graffiti artist.

We are going to stay with Anthony and India, and I am looking forward to the sound of the sea at their front door. We will talk about my father's retirement and how he fills his days with walks, food, reading and little else. We will talk about their sons: Tim's life as an oboe player in a London orchestra; Alex's as an accountant in New York. India will sigh because her children choose to live so far away. Anthony will rant about the latest inaccurate research on seaweed that he has read in some magazine or on the Internet. He will expect me to understand and share his rage over a minor mistake. Seaweed is all; he won't have it messed with. I will play along.

Cormac pulls off the motorway at Ballinasloe so we can eat. He brings Nessa into a hotel to change her nappy and I wait outside. The town is quiet and many of the shops are vacant, their windows whited-out. I watch a young mother push a buggy with a lumpen three-year-old in it; the child is swilling on a bottle of fizzy orange and her fringe is cut that little bit too short. Cormac steps out of the hotel and we cross the road to the café my family always used to stop at when Anthony and Verity brought us to Galway on holidays. It is on the square and the same people are in it, drinking pint glasses of milk and eating big Irish dinners at noon: spuds, beef and turnip; slabs of gammon topped with pineapple; generous shepherd's pies.

'It even smells the same,' I say to Cormac, as we take our seats, 'like a farmer's kitchen.' I inspect the glass cabinet of cakes. 'Me and Robin were always allowed to have black forest gâteau here – the pinnacle of luxury.'

Three staff separately try to take our order before we have decided what we want. The café is under renovation and it is cold. At intervals, the sound of hammering is as noisy as set dancers thumping across the floor. A framed GAA shirt in bumblebee colours is the only decoration on the walls. People know each other here; they shout greetings across the room. An old woman limps towards the exit, gripping each table she passes; a younger woman comes behind her, saying, 'Are you OK, Mammy? Can you manage?'

'You can fuckin' bury me before I'll use a stick,' the elderly woman says to me. The daughter rolls her eyes and grins.

We eat BLTs and, under a shawl, I feed Nessa. Her arm, the only visible part of her, pokes upwards every so often in a victory salute. When she is finished feeding, I lift the shawl off her face and she smiles like someone returned after a long trip. Cormac flicks through a discarded copy of *The Star* and I watch a waitress carefully fold cutlery into paper napkins. The woman behind the counter hands a chocolate bun to every child in the place, just as she did when I was a kid. It makes me wonder when Nessa will be deemed big enough to accept her free treat.

'Would you like something nice with your tea?' the waiter asks, when he clears our plates.

'Oh, I might have a dessert, yes.'

'Sure why wouldn't you?' he says, petting Nessa's cheek as if she is his own and going to get menus for us.

I look around at the well-filled women and men, stuffed behind their tables, eating alone and in pairs. I feel, suddenly, like I am making the slow trip back to myself and I grab Cormac's hand across the table and kiss it.

'I love you, babe,' he says, something he does aloud, unabashed and often.

'I love you too.'

The waiter brings me an oblong doughnut, bulky with piped cream and topped with a slick of red.

'Wow,' Cormac says, 'it's like someone cut their finger and dripped blood onto the cake.'

'Mmm, let me at it.'

Cormac has a coffee slice with tan icing. We gobble our way through the cakes, marvelling with stuffed mouths at how good they taste.

'So retro,' he says, picking gluey pastry from his teeth.

'I'll be Bessie Bunter after this.'

'It's your birthday, Lil – anything goes.'

When we step outside the café the sun is shining; Cormac carries Nessa and we stroll across the square to explore a tat and toy shop. Cormac shoves a white sun hat with a floral ribbon onto my head, then goes to the till to pay for it. The owner of the shop is from Dublin too and Cormac flirts with her in that unconscious, low-key way he has, asking what part she is from and how long she has lived in Ballinasloe. The woman tickles Nessa and grins at Cormac; I step in to claim my place with them.

'Are you going to say hello, Nessa?' I say, leaning in to look at her face. She gives a wet, gummy grin and sticks one fist in her mouth.

'She's a pet. Gorgeous,' the shopkeeper says, and we all smile. 'Enjoy yourselves inside in the city now.'

We leave, me with the sun hat still on and, this being Galway, by the time we get back to our car it is raining again.

We pull up at my father's virgin blue door; the sun is back, fighting to shrug off clouds. I see Anthony at the window and he is soon outside with India, the pair of them crowding around the passenger door to get a hold of Nessa. Anthony unstraps the baby and cradles her. He and India have their backs to us while they fuss over her; we take our luggage from the boot. Remembering themselves, they turn around; India embraces Cormac, while Anthony kisses my cheek.

'All right, darling?' Anthony says.

'Grand. How are you both?'

'Tipping away. You brought the good weather.'

'We try,' Cormac says, hefting our bags through the door.

They wish me a happy birthday and I slip into the window seat and look at the river; a yellow traffic cone bobs past, chasing a mallard who looks very addled and put out. The swans are over the other side of the basin, flocking to where people throw food for them. A green boat called *Cú na Mara* sits by the end of Nimmo's Pier.

'Let's go for a pint,' Anthony says, rubbing his hands together.

'It's too early for me, Dad. Cormac would have a pint though, right?'

'Sure.'

They head off, Anthony delighted to have a man to drink with, giddy because India is letting him go to the pub in the afternoon. He says they will only have the one.

India stands in the middle of the floor, holding Nessa, rocking her. We are easier now than we used to be, but there is something residual still – the whiff of the other woman off her that refuses to budge, even after twenty-five years. We are less inclined to long silences but, with the baby to goo over, there is little reason to talk. Nessa smiles and drools; she wiggles her legs and India grabs at her feet and admires her striped tights. The baby grips India's dark finger in her pink fist and tries to suck her nail; India offers her a knuckle instead.

'I would have loved to have had a baby girl,' she says.

'Boys are brilliant too.'

I blush fiercely and India notices it; she cocks her head. 'Maybe you will have a boy next.'

'Ah, no; I won't be having any more babies, I'm too old. Too old, too tired, too broke.'

I turn away, hoping my scalding face will right itself. An image of Malachy floats across my vision and I put my palm against my handbag, where I now carry the picture of the two of us from the hospital in Glasgow.

'How is your mother?'

'Great. She's getting ready for a new exhibition at The Rubicon.'

'And Robin?'

'Well, according to his Facebook page, he's in Spain.'

'And Verity likes being a grandmother, does she?'

'She's perfecting the art. Slowly.'

India laughs and perches on the arm of the sofa. 'Nessa, you are such a good baby. Your uncles cried and cried and cried when they were little.'

'Did they? Poor you.' The workings of other people's children interest me now like they never did.

'We called my grandmother "Grammy". Might Nessa call me "Grammy India"?'

She looks anxious and I can see this means something to her; a lot, maybe.

'Of course.' I smile. 'Grammy India, it is. She's very content in your arms, I must say.'

She holds Nessa up and whooshes her through the air in a way that alarms me. I want to tell her to stop but I remember her doing the same with Tim and Alex when they were small and they turned out all right.

'Whee-shah,' India sings, sailing the baby up and down, 'wheeeee-shah.'

Nessa laughs in a way I have never heard before, a sustained rolling gurgle – it is pure glee. I watch India and think what a good mother she has always been to her boys. I remember how she tried her best with Robin and me though I, at least, resented her with an outrage that bordered on hatred. While she is playing with Nessa, I sneak a look at the picture of Malachy and me, half-sliding it out of my handbag, smiling at it, then stuffing it back in.

When I look up, India is watching me, with that same questioning stare she wore when she noticed me blush.

'Let's have coffee,' she says. 'Anthony got me a ridiculous cappuccino machine. Why don't you help me get it going?'

I can't sleep; I am not used to wine anymore and my throbbing head keeps me awake. I slip from the bed and roll up the bamboo blind. The water in the Claddagh basin is dark and the moon is shy, lifting her hem to flash only a slice of brightness. A streetlight throws its sodium fuzz onto the slates of the church on the other side of the pier. I crane my neck to see if I can see the swans; I wonder where they go at night.

Cormac stirs and comes to stand behind me. He slips his arms around my waist and softly sings a line from a song we like into my ear, telling me to look up and he'll meet me at the moon. We sway together at the window, my back flush to his chest. I feel his cock harden; he cups my breasts and kisses my neck. I turn to him and we kiss, slow and long. Soon, we are back under the covers.

'I'll be listening to the moon song when you're in Scotland,' Cormac whispers. 'I'll miss you.'

His hand moves over my hips and into my knickers; he catches his thumb into the side and slips them off. We kiss, gliding our tongues over each other's lips and then plunging deeper. He slides on top of me and slowly, slowly enters me. I gasp and we move together, giggling when the headboard thumps and the bed whines rhythmically under us. Cormac rams the headboard against the wall with one hand to keep it quiet. And on we go.

Chapter Ten

My stomach is stuck to my back with the hunger, but I can't eat. I poke at the smoked salmon on my plate, lifting its fat edges to watch its colour change from purple to silver to orange. I butter a wedge of bread, take a few bites and suddenly feel as full as an egg. There is a woman sitting across from me, spooning prawn cocktail into her mouth with gusto; she only stops gulping it down long enough to sip from a huge glass of red wine. She is thin, sick looking, and I sit worrying about her digestion. She makes no mess, I notice, with the Marie Rose sauce; none of it falls into her dainty lap or oozes from the corners of her mouth. I begin to fret less about her; she is all right, she has it together.

On the other side of me a man in a smart suit clips his nails with his teeth and spits the leavings into the air; I want to smack him, or at least tell him to stop. He is making me feel queasy so I turn away and watch the door. I look at the street through the window: urban roses nod their heads in troughs on the pub's windowsill, made heavy by their own scent, maybe, and by exhaust fumes. On the way in I noticed the pub had turrets, of all things, and I fantasise about sitting in one and watching the comings and goings on the street below like a fairytale prisoner. The pub is called 'The Fox and Thistle' and there is a poorly mounted fox in a glass case behind the bar; Verity would spit feathers if she could see how high his ears sit and the way his eyes swing outwards. My God, I am getting as bad as her. I tap my fingers and swill spit around my cotton mouth to loosen it up; I drink from my glass of Coke but it clogs my throat. I cough and sniff. Am I getting a cold?

When they finally arrive I am rummaging in my handbag for a tissue and I completely miss their entrance. They stand over me and the woman is smiling. I fuss to my feet, knocking against my glass with my bag, and she grabs me into a hug, then stands too close. She is still grinning at me, as if she has achieved something great and hopes that I will acknowledge it.

'Lillis,' she says. 'At last.'

'Tanya.' I pump her hand. 'And Mal,' I say, turning to him; I feel like some fool on a blind date. He waves, blushes, then takes my hand in his. I press both mine around his fingers until he pulls away, hitches his hoodie at the waistband and sits.

Tanya questions me in that way that makes you know you have been discussed and found worthy – she is open to me, and seems to will me to perform to her liking. There is a maniacal quality to her eagerness to hear what I am going to say next. It is flattering, somehow, but I also feel like I am being quizzed and I am not one hundred per cent sure if my answers are right. Still, when I speak, she nods, smiles and glances at Mal, and I keep thinking she is going to reach over and caress my cheek, or put her head on my shoulder and cry. Her eyes glisten with ready-to-drop tears. The questions are unending: Was my plane trip over OK? *It was.* Did I hire a car? *I did.* Do I like my job? *I do.* Are my parents still living? *They are.* Is Dublin my hometown? *It is.*

She tells me that her husband – Mal's Dad, Ian – is away on business and hopes to meet me sometime soon.

'Here or in Ireland,' she says. 'We could come over.'

'Oh,' I say, feeling as if I am being pulled at a gallop to a place I am not altogether sure I want to go.

'Are you…' she hesitates, 'in a relationship?'

'I'm married. Recently married. Well, two years ago.'

Mal says nothing but his eyes drink me in; I want to stare at him, make sense of him, take in every detail of him, but I am rigid with nerves. I fidget with my handbag strap, twist a curl around one finger; I even poke my fingers into my ears, for God's sake. I notice that Tanya's helmet of dark hair doesn't move when she moves. I look at Mal and look away; I look again. He has Struan's frame and face, my hair – not dark like Struan's was when he was young, but fair. His hands are feminine: he has slim, tapered fingers; neat, blunt nails; his skin is tanned. He is quiet.

Tanya speaks again and I notice for the first time that she lisps attractively, adding a sibilance to her 's' words that sounds childish and charming, though she must be in her mid-fifties.

'So, did you have any more kids, Lillis? *Do* you have more?'

'I have a daughter. Nessa. She's four months old.'

'Four months. Imagine!' Tanya says, looking at Mal. 'Nessa is a pretty name. You name well.'

As I say Nessa's name, my breasts tingle and I feel milk surge; I fold my arms across my chest and press hard so that I won't leak. But the let-down has started. I jump up, excuse myself and go to the pub's bathroom. In the cubicle, I fold loo roll into wads and slip them into my bra. How could I have forgotten to wear breast pads? Stupid, stupid, stupid. In the mirror over the sink I look hunted and strained. And something else – frightened, maybe. There is a taste in my mouth; my tongue is as bitter as burnt toast. I pull a packet of Polo mints from my bag and crunch one quickly; I neaten my hair and rub my finger over my teeth.

Tanya stands up as I approach the table. 'I'm going to leave you two alone,' she says. Then, 'The weather is beautiful,' as if the sunshine is something she has gifted to me, gifted to the world.

She squeezes Mal's shoulder as she moves behind his chair and smiles hugely. I look at him and wonder if he has been coddled and cosseted all of his life, the way only children often are. I wonder if he had difficult teens. Was there ever a maelstrom in him, or was he always as becalmed as he seems now? Surely every youngster has their sullen, sulky, monosyllabic spell. Or did Tanya and Ian do such a great job that Mal stayed on an even keel, untroubled by hormonal storms? I feel the push of jealousy at the thought. Still, sitting beside him aerates me; every part of me feels more able, stronger, settled. But giddy too.

'So I have a wee sister,' Mal says, when Tanya is gone out the door.

'A half sister, yes.'

Mal winces and I am not sure why on earth I made that distinction.

'Do you have any snaps of her?'

'Sure.' I take my digital camera from my bag and watch as he arrows silently through the pictures of Nessa – they are all that are on it. He takes his time, studies Nessa's face. I wonder what he sees in her tiny, serene features. 'She's so new; she relearns the world every day.'

'She's bonny,' he says.

'An angel.'

'I was a demon, according to my mother,' Mal says, and the word mother hangs between us like a sprite, flickering out after a few moments but not until we are both squirming.

'Well, I was a demon too, apparently,' I say, eventually, and lift my glass to sip at the dregs of Coke. 'The paperweight arrived in one piece, you'll be glad to hear.'

'Good, I'm glad. I wanted you to get it on my birthday. Did you?'

'I did. I always think of you that day. I think of you all the time.'

He nods and looks down at his runners. 'And I think of you.'

'The paperweight belonged to Struan, your birth father.'

'I know.'

I set down my glass. 'How do you know that?'

'I knew Struan all my life, pretty much.'

'What? Oh. Really?' I consider this. 'You said you "knew" him?'

'He died two summers ago. Lung cancer.'

I recede into my own head and something clicks in my throat. 'Oh, my God.' I rub my forehead. 'Were you close?' I whisper.

'Sort of. We met up a couple of times a year, here or in Kinlochbrack. He told me all about you.'

'All about me.'

What Mal has said churns me up but I need to put it to one side, to concentrate on him during our small, precious time together. I ask about his life with his parents, with friends. He talks about Crieff, that it is quiet but he likes it; about how most of his pals went off to Glasgow and Dundee to university, but he stayed to work in his Dad's timber yard. He shrugs as he says it and I'm not sure what to take from that.

'Did you have to stay?'

'I love the yard but sometimes I wonder if I should have gone to uni. Just to try it.'

'What would you have studied?'

'I don't know. Art, maybe.'

My heart jumps. 'My mother is an artist. I'm a photographer.'

There is effort in my voice as we chat, though I am extraordinarily happy to be sitting in this pub, in this small Scottish town, talking with Malachy. It feels like the oddest conversation of my life and I flounder from one thing to the next, hardly daring to draw breath in case I run out of things to say. He tells me he plays guitar badly and I detect this is modesty, while I imagine him perched on his bed, his head bent low, watching his fingers pick and strum.

I ask if I can photograph him and he nods. I take a few pictures quickly: *flash flash flash*. A smatter of sunlight falls through the window across Mal's hair, making it glow. He is beautiful, my son, and his Scottish accent sends me spinning as I listen to him talk. In all the years I have been imagining this reunion I have never heard his voice in anything but a Dublin accent. It seems so stupid now, but there you have it; I can be a very stupid woman at times.

I listen to Lady Ga Ga as I drive north, away from Crieff, and grow to love her voice; she starts to sound as recognisable and comforting to me as a friend. Right at the end of one track, the burble of a didgeridoo cradles me in its long, anticipative tone, matching my mood perfectly.

It is a hot, blue-sky day. The good weather is a blessing – I hate travelling unfamiliar roads in rain – and the hazy sunshine makes everything look smooth: the hills, the signs, and the fields of golden rape that bracket the road. It is odd to be driving by myself, with no Cormac or Nessa. Usually Cormac takes the wheel and I sit in the back. He treats driving as a solvable puzzle, whereas I go at it like a battering ram. I am a bad navigator and a poor follower of instructions too so, when I'm alone, I plunge forward, mapless, hoping for good signposts.

The road to Inverness has changed in twenty years and I barely remember it anyway, but it is straightforward; there is no opportunity to get lost or take a wrong turn. Cows, just like Irish cows, bask in the sun and the sheep are woollying up already after their spring shearing. Windmills sit on slopes like enormous candles on a cake; their blades cut the horizon, moving lethargically in the still summer air. I pass sweet, hilly villages with musical names: Lochty, Huntingtower, Logiealmond. Iceland trucks drag their orange glow ahead of my car and behind it too.

I feel the backward pull to Crieff as I move further away from it; I have a thousand more things to discuss with Mal, a million more. I go over every word that passed between us and guess the *Why?* he must ask will come later. And what do I tell him? That I come from a line of unsuccessful mothers and that I did not think he deserved to be mothered by the next one? That Struan and I were incompatible? I wonder how much Mal knows. I wonder what Struan told him about me, about us. It galls me now to think that Struan knew our son and I didn't. Why did he not contact me or try to draw me back?

I think about the fact that Malachy looks a lot like Robin at the same age, but he is composed, on a more even keel than my brother was, it seems to me. I feel sick and skittish; I want to turn the car around and go back to him. I want to talk and listen and explain. But I also need to go to Kinlochbrack.

The road that leads to it is gentle – it is wide enough for two cars, and is flanked by dog daisies and pink rhododendron. It runs by peaks and lakes, past a reservoir and the odd cluster of holiday cottages. The roadkill is more exotic than at home: I see a fawn and a bird of prey along with the wrecked carcasses that were once hedgehogs and cats. Verity would want to stop and haul them into the car, of course; the thought makes me smile.

All of Kinlochbrack village is bathed in Sunday quiet; I park the car on Shore Street and walk. The Caledonian MacBrayne ferry still hulks in the harbour, the biggest thing to fill the sightline apart from the hills and the loch itself. The Klondykers are long gone. Kinlochbrack looks smaller and yet, oddly, bigger than my memory allows; I can't explain or understand it. The streets, though they occupy the same grid that they have for over two hundred years, confuse me. How did Clanranald Street get *there*? Was Market Street always this long? I take photographs as I walk, surprised by how acquainted I begin to feel with each scene; it feels like groping in a dark room that is slowly being saturated with light.

I make my way towards the Strathcorry Inn and it squats, a long white jumble of buildings, with lavender and ferns in pots under the windows. I sit outside with a cup of tea; I see a grey-haired man with a beard who could be Kenny; I see a woman I recognise from the inn's laundry who looks healthier than she did twenty years ago. I see another man, his red-raddled face a result, maybe, of years of drinking. He looks familiar to me the way everyone is suddenly familiar. Even the hill walkers in their top-notch fleeces and boots are like the hill walkers who always gathered outside the inn to eat and drink on fine days.

I order a glass of Syrah from the waitress who has an Antipodean lilt to her voice – more familiarity. She brings me salted almonds in a ramekin; I crunch them and sip the wine while listening to one Englishman bore another Englishman with an account of a sailing trip he took to Malta. The quiet one drinks faster than his companion and he catches my eye and winks.

In truth, I don't know what I am doing sitting outside the Strathcorry Inn, watching everyone who passes; I feel I am trying to grasp at a group of ghosts who have left no imprint. And how could they have? How could *I* have left any trace? Everything is turned around. I go into the Strathcorry and walk through. The rooms are divided differently – the gallery now sits off the bistro, the reception is larger yet everything seems small, so small. The staff are friendly and seem content but, without Struan, the place feels all wrong.

My B&B smells of damp drowned in air-freshener; it makes me gag. It is one of those places that has signs everywhere telling you what *not* to do. 'Do not smoke in the bedrooms'; 'Do not wear outdoor shoes indoors'; 'Do not have the TV volume loud after 9pm'. 9pm! I don't feel welcome and I have the privilege of paying for my intrusion.

185

Maybe that is the way it is in most B&Bs. The landlady acts surprised every time I open the door and walk in.

'Oh,' she says, 'you're here.' As if she would prefer that I were not.

'Yes, only me,' I say, or some other foolishness.

I had been hoping for a gossipy old dear who I could quiz about everyone I used to know in the village. But, the view is good from my room. I can see the last hills along Loch Brack before it opens its maw to the sea; and the water, of course, which lies smooth and grey until the ferry ploughs through it, crashing waves against the shore that I can hear from my bed. And there are white roses under my window – roses as big as a child's head – and their smell is intoxicating.

I go outside and take some of the photographs I was sent to take for the newspaper. Of the sea, the loch, the white and black houses, the seals, the boats in the harbour, wheeling seagulls against cloud, of the Gàidhlig street signs, and the mountains stacked one behind the other like cut-outs in five shades of blue. I stand in front of Struan's house on Clanranald Street and look at the upstairs window where a net curtain billows, just as it did twenty years ago. I walk through the village and imagine a different life for myself; a life where I stayed and settled and brought up Malachy as my own. Mine and Struan's.

From my B&B room I ring Verity. My hands are slick and shaking and my mobile phone slips from my fingers like a live salmon. I wipe it with the edge of the sheet and when my mother answers, I manage to whisper that it is me. I start to sob.

'Ah now. Stop that, Lillis. Nessa is fine. I know you miss her but she's grand. She's sucking away on a bottle as we speak. Listen.'

I hear Nessa's little suckles and the sounds of the milk hitting her throat; my breasts fill and I press against them with both elbows.

'I do miss her; I miss her like mad.' I gulp and wipe away snot with a sopping tissue. 'Mam, I need to tell you something. It's important.'

'Go on.'

'Well, it's hard to know how to put it. I, well, it's that you have a twenty-year-old grandson in Scotland. My son. I had a baby. I've met him; I met up with him yesterday in Crieff.'

Verity sighs hugely and my phone slides again. She says something that I don't catch and I grip the mobile and shove it to my ear.

'The phone fell. What's that? What did you say?'

'I said I know, sweetheart. I know about your first baby. I've always known.'

Her answer bullets over the phone line and lodges in my brain. My hands shake and my ribs bend outwards like they will snap, then they contract. 'You know? You *knew*?"

'I knew.' She sighs again.

'What? I can't believe that you knew, all that time. All those years.'

'How could I *not* know? I took one look at you coming into the arrivals hall at the airport and I knew. Well, at first I thought you were pregnant still, but I realised after a while what must have happened.'

'You never said a thing.' It shocks me that she could have known and said nothing. Absolutely nothing. For twenty years! Who does that? What kind of a woman does that to her own daughter, leaves her to deal, alone, with the hugeness of such a thing? My blood seems to fizz through my veins and it makes my head and limbs pop. 'Jesus, I could have done with you saying something, Mam. Anything.'

'Could you? You didn't seem like a person who wanted that conversation. At the time.'

I try to fathom this. Verity knew the truth about me but chose silence because she thought that was what I wanted. 'But I can't believe you didn't bring it up. *Ever.*'

'But neither did you, sweetheart.'

'I didn't know how to; I was all over the place. You could have said something later. Any time. You know, when I had my miscarriage. Or when I was expecting Nessa.'

'What? And upset you when you were already vulnerable? By then it was up to you, Lillis. If I had cracked that egg you would have turned your back on me. You know you would.'

She sounds so sure but I am not sure. I stuck by her through every sort of name-calling and disaster; I pulled her back to herself time and time over. I am stunned that through years of abusing me she didn't

187

manage to toss this one thing at me: that I was a mother, and that I had abandoned my child.

'Still,' I say, wanting her to know that I blame her. I want, too, to be properly angry with her. But meeting Mal has caused a freshness to rush through me, a vigour, and it has softened my edges. What went before doesn't matter as much now that I have seen him and talked to him and, in a way, confirmed for myself that he is real.

I hold the mobile away from my face and look at it, as if Verity might spirit through the speaker and sit on my B&B bed in Kinlochbrack and explain herself. And if she does, that I might be able to forgive her. She coughs and I put the phone to my ear.

'I am sorry, you know,' she says. 'I did a lot wrong and I'm sorry. I worried about what happened, over the years; I worried about you.'

'Does Dad know about it? Robin?'

'I never said a thing.' I look out the window at the nodding white roses and beyond them to the sea loch. 'What's his name, your son?' Verity's voice is gentle.

'Malachy Dónal. He's known as Mal.'

'Lillis, listen to me. Don't fuck this up. Do you hear me? You have everything you've ever wanted now. Jump at the sun, sweetheart. Don't be like me. Jump at the sun.'

Fashioned in wrought iron, over the gate to the tiny Catholic graveyard at the end of Market Street, are the words, 'May all who rest here feel content'. Bees drone around my ears and white butterflies toss themselves through the air unsure, it seems, which direction to take. My shoes crackle noisily on the gravel path, so I walk on the grass verge instead. Struan's grave is tucked by the far wall, high enough up for a view of Loch Brack but sheltered all the same. Malachy told me where to find it. The gravestone is white marble; it has Struan's name and dates and a Celtic scroll. I lift my camera to take a picture then stop; some things are better not photographed.

Among the white stones covering the plot, I arrange the finds from a morning's beachcombing on the strand below the B&B: a piece of pale sea glass with a zippered ridge; bits of sea pottery

– blue and red willow pattern chips with edges as smooth as bone; an eardrum shell; slices of mother of pearl; a scatter of winkles; and a wedge of green glass with the letters STER, which I try, and fail, to pluck some meaning from. I finger a mussel shell which was given to me by a boy on the beach – he was the only other person there. He tapped me on the arm, startling me, and held up a perfect sea urchin for me to admire.

'Wow, that's very beautiful,' I said, 'weren't you lucky?'

'For you,' he said, and handed me not the urchin but a mussel shell. He stared at it in my palm as if he didn't want to let it go.

'Thank you,' I said, 'that's lovely,' and he shambled away. There was something wandering in the boy, in his carry-on, in his eye. He is somebody's son, I thought, watching him walk along the beach alone, dipping down to fish some new treasure from among the pebbles.

'For you,' I say now, as I place the mussel shell at the top of Struan's grave, under the headstone. Struan, whose heart was as well hidden as a plover's egg on a stony beach. Struan who gave me *my* son. 'Goodbye, Struan,' I say, 'and thank you.'

I left Kinlochbrack the last time on a cold evening. The moon was riding high over the loch, throwing an unnaturally bright light onto the water; it was a huge cratered ball, glowing yellow in the black. As the bus pulled away from the harbour, I kept my eyes on the moon, so I wouldn't have to see the village as I left it behind.

Today the sun shines as I drive along Shore Street and Loch Brack shimmers under the prawn boats being emptied by boy-fishermen in Day-Glo wellies. I go past the pier where a policeman directs the traffic that rumbles out of the belly of the ferry; he stops the cars to let me drive on. I drive past The Windhorse, which still survives with its beauty board walls and Clan MacLeod carpet inside. I pass the house that holds a row of bronze heads in its window: a stern man, a young boy and a foetal-faced baby, caught in an eternity of staring over the loch. I pass the graveyard that holds Struan's body. And on I drive, up past the Braes and on towards Beinn Dearg which is under a lid of moss-stitch cloud. I overtake cyclists, bright in red jackets, their heavy panniers making them wobble as they tackle the uphill slopes. On the roadside there are lambs so cuddly I want to stop the car and hug them. For nearly six hours I drive south, on and on.

My aeroplane lands late. I walk into the arrivals hall at Dublin airport and I see a family stringing a banner between them: 'Welcome to your new home, Baby Anna'. Pink balloons billow from either end. Their faces are creased with excitement, these new grannies, cousins and uncles who wait for Anna, who is probably coming to them from Russia or Vietnam. The first thing that pops into my mind is how unbelievably fortunate this baby is, to be welcomed with such love, with such giddy warmth, into her new family.

Cormac stands to one side of the banner with Nessa in his arms. He grins and waves and I rush forward. I kiss Cormac and pull Nessa into my own arms; I swear she has grown bigger in the five days I have been away. But I am back now to mother her, to be the mother that I am capable of being. And Kinlochbrack is a place of memories. That is all.

BOOK CLUB QUESTIONS

The Closet of Savage Mementos is a narrative about grief, betrayal by loved ones, motherhood, loss, post-natal depression and the grip of past events. The novel examines how the past influences the present and how secrets cannot be ignored. But ultimately it is a book of hope: Lillis is determined not to become the mother her mother was, so she gives up her son for adoption. She is forced into examining this decision when she has another baby twenty years later. Lillis's hope is to be a good mother to her daughter, but she has to go back to the past, to the son she gave away, in order to find out how to become the mother she wants to be.

Is Verity a bad mother?

Is Lillis a good daughter?

Does Lillis's initial decision not to be a mother reflect her experience of Verity as a mother?

Does the novel answer the question: does poor parenting cause poor parenting, or a fear of being a parent?

The Irish family is represented in different ways in the novel – Lillis's separated parents, her father's new family, the Spain family. What is the author trying to say about families in Irish society?

How is grief portrayed in the novel? Are there different kinds of grief in the book?

Is the age gap between Lillis and Struan relevant to their poor communication skills with each other?

Why does Struan betray Lillis?

Does Robin also betray Lillis?

Why did Lillis not let Struan know about her pregnancy?

Are there reasons that Struan does not attempt to contact Lillis after she leaves Kinlochbrack?

Why did Verity not tackle Lillis about what really happened to her in Scotland?

Are the friendships in the book good friendships? Think of Lillis and Dónal; Lillis and Margaret; Struan and Sam; Robin and Fidelma.

The narrative is about grief and love and how the two become entwined with unpredictable results. How is this handled?

In what ways does the past influence the present in the novel?

How important is the fact that Verity is a professional artist to Lillis's desire to be a photographer?

Objects (paperweights and shells) and icons (the Virgin Mary) appear frequently. What is their significance? Do they add to the reader's experience?

What does Cormac represent in the novel?

Is Cormac a replacement for Dónal, or a better version of him?

Are the sex scenes in the book well executed?

How does the depiction of post-natal depression – and Lillis's unravelling – affect the reader?

Which of the characters is the easiest to identify with?

What role does landscape play in the novel?

Do Scotland and Ireland come off differently in the book? Is one place shown in a more attractive light than the other?

How does the future look for Lillis, Mal and Nessa? Will she able to mother her children well?

If you would like to ask the author any questions about the novel, you can contact her at nuala@nualanichonchuir.com